Return item

DEATH PAINTS THE PICTURE

Graphic artist and true-crime buff Homer Bull is always looking for a good murder for his syndicated comic strip. He just never expected to be invited to one — courtesy of his old pal Hugo Shipley. When Shipley himself drops dead from an apparent self-inflicted gunshot wound, it's no laughing matter. Everyone but Homer is quick to accept the suicide bunk. Maybe that's because everyone but Homer has their own sordid secrets and motives. And not one of them is leaving Shipley's isolated estate before Homer finds his friend's killer.

LAWRENCE LARIAR

DEATH PAINTS THE PICTURE

Complete and Unabridged

LINFORD
Leicester

First published in Great Britain

First Linford Edition
published 2019

A catalogue record for this book is available
from the British Library.

ISBN 978–1–4448–4268–5

Published by
F. A. Thorpe (Publishing)
Anstey, Leicestershire

Set by Words & Graphics Ltd.
Anstey, Leicestershire
Printed and bound in Great Britain by
T. J. International Ltd., Padstow, Cornwall

This book is printed on acid-free paper

1

Invitation to a Party

Nobody but me, Hank MacAndrews, would ever have bothered with the Cheruckten Courthouse (and Town Hall).

I bothered because I had to bother. Homer wanted a sketch of it, and I couldn't very well disappoint him. Homer is that way — a fiend about detail, atmosphere, and background. Homer is stubborn. I'm stubborn, too. So I do as Homer says. Eighty-five potatoes per week is a tidy sum. It clothes me at Finchley's, feeds me steak and onions when I crave them, and keeps Mrs. McCrory, my lantern-jawed landlady, at a congenial distance.

My sketch was not art. Any good high school student could have done as well. The Cheruckten Courthouse was nothing more than a glorified barn with a small gagged-up turret of some sort pasted on the roof. In the old days, I assumed, there must have been a reason for ringing the bell in that turret.

The building itself had been white-washed long ago, but now the dirty walls almost lost themselves in the deeper grey of the sky beyond, and only the lacy black of branches against the sides gave it contour and solidity. It was strictly a Thomas Benton courthouse. He could have it. I shivered and blew my nose again.

Somebody tapped me on the shoulder. I turned to face a messenger youth.

'You Bisteh Bull?' the stuffed-up, sniffling boy asked, and held out a telegram.

'Practically,' I muttered, grabbing for the message.

He jerked it away with a toothy grin. 'Collect — two bucks twenny!'

'Oh,' said I. 'You want Mr. Bull. You'll find him in the courthouse, probably talking to the woman at the desk.'

He edged past me up the wooden steps, and I whipped out my pad and sketched a quick memory blob of his weasel face. It would come in handy someday, when the comic strip lacked a zombie. All our zombies had to be drawn from nature.

That was Homer's method. Homer Bull was a demon data fiend. All his material always came straight from life — straight from actual courts. His daily comic strip, *True Stories of Crime*, was built on that premise. 'I don't like a fiction murder,' Homer would say. 'I don't want Sherlock Holmes or Father Brown or the drawing room patter of Hercule Poirot. There can never be anything quite so impossible as simplicity. Let a simple soul do a job of murder, and we've got four weeks of smooth flowing comic strip continuity without any effort.'

Well, the effort was all Homer's. I did only the cartooning. Homer wrote the stuff, transformed it from dry rot of the courthouse files to the daily drama of the comic strip. And Homer knew how. His syndicate records proved it. *True Stories of Crime* now ran in three hundred papers, with new customers added every week.

More than once, Wilkinson of the

Brooklyn police had made use of his talents. But the real build-up for Homer came after the schoolgirl murders on Church Avenue. He broke the case on his own, and the newspapers raved him into sudden fame. Ever on the alert for a pot shot at Dame Fortune, Homer signed with Queen Features Syndicate for a trial of *True Stories of Crime*. The rest is comic strip history.

The courthouse door opened and out came Homer, wriggling his fat frame into his overcoat. He minced down the steps and faced me in the gloom.

'The old heckty-peckty,' he sighed, handing me the wire, 'Heckty-peckty from the Shtunk.'

I read the telegram. It was a typical Shtunk Smith masterpiece.

I AM JUST BACK FROM BINGE STOP FOUND INVITATION TO WEEKEND PARTY GINK NAMED SHIPLEY STOP SHOULD HAVE OPENED THIS ITEM LAST FRIDAY BUT ON ACCOUNT ABOVE BINGE DIDN'T STOP SEE THIS MORNING AFTER PAPER FOR STUFF STOP

ALSO SOME MUG CALLING YOU ON
PHONE ALL THE TIME FOR YOU PER-
SONAL STOP BETTER COME BACK
QUICK SEE YOU LATER

SHTUNK

'A masterpiece of innuendo,' I said.

Homer grinned. 'You finished with your sketches?' I nodded. 'Then we're off, Hank. This Shipley business interests me — and those calls might be from the syndicate, you know.'

I knew. Homer had promised Queen Features an outline of his next plot. We were a little behind in our schedule.

The train steamed in, finally, and we hopped aboard.

'Goodbye, Cheruckten,' I bronxed through my chapped lips.

Homer's expert nose had already detected the way to the bar. There was a bar, and a bartender with a hearty laugh and plenty of antidote for Cheruckten weather. We attacked a jug of Bourbon until Homer's nose turned from light blue to pastel pink and then glowed like a traffic light, complete with highlights.

'I wonder about the Shtunk,' mused Homer, fingering his glass.

I gulped another hooker. 'You should wonder? For two cents a word you'd find the reason quickly enough, you Hemingway, you.'

But Homer was lost in thought. 'It must be something mighty important. It had better be. I told Shtunk that I wasn't to be disturbed.' He called the bartender. 'Got a morning paper, George?'

George had eight. Seven were from below the Mason-Dixon Line, and the eighth was an old issue of *Women's Wear*. The barman explained that we would pick up a New York paper at the next station. There was a long silence punctuated by the glug of whiskey pouring.

'Let me see that wire, Hank?'

I leaned it against the bottle of Bourbon. Homer studied it intently.

'He just got back from a binge,' Homer translated. 'And he found an invitation to a weekend at Hugo Shipley's place.' He turned to me. 'You know who Shipley is, of course?'

6

'I read the tabloids occasionally, chum.'

'He goes on to say that I should be up at Shipley's for some reason I'll find in this morning's paper. Now what in the world could have happened at Shipley's that'd interest me?'

'He's been known to have fancy peep shows occasionally,' I suggested.

'Nonsense! Hugo Shipley doesn't know me well enough for that.'

It was amazing, sometimes, how flat my quips could fall. Or was it only that Homer didn't bother to laugh? He looked positively sad, suddenly.

'You're not worried?' I asked. 'Not worried about Shipley, are you?'

'Don't be a fool.' He massaged his eyebrow. 'I have an idea that Shipley is up to one of his practical jokes again. I think I know why he wanted me there.'

I had a pretty good idea, too. But I couldn't mention it. It was too obvious.

'I'm pretty sure Hugo's crowd includes Douglas Trum, Hank,' said Homer. 'If Trum is up there this weekend, I can put two and two together and get — ' He turned to me for the answer.

'Grace?'

'For a cartoonist, you think clearly,' Homer sighed. 'Of course little Grace is there. And where Grace is . . . '

I filled his glass and kept my trap shut. Love is a kick in the pants.

2

Shtunk Smith

Homer was funny that way — about Grace, I mean. Give him a couple of stiff snorts and wait for that faraway look. Over the river and far away looked Homer. Through the wall and into the next county looked Homer. Homer just looked, but I knew what he was mooing about. When Homer mooed, everybody knew why.

It was Grace.

Everybody knew all about Grace, long before Homer met her and married her in the dark days of '32 when love was a bigger gamble than the stock market. Who can understand the vagaries of women? Who can figure why Grace married Homer or why Homer married Grace, for that matter? Homer was nobody's fool, even though he was starving to death. He earned his bread with very little butter — in those days. He was a gagman, feeding funny little lines to the horde of cartoonists who decorate the back pages of *Collier's* and the *Saturday Evening Post* with their whimsy. And Homer was a good gagman, even though he starved.

But maybe Grace wasn't so dumb. She must have known that he wouldn't wander in the quagmire of professional humor for long. Maybe she knew that Homer's fertile brain was already plumbing the mysteries of fiction and radio writing, and any other type of storytelling that paid through the nose. For Homer was anxious to forget the willy-nilly life of a gagman.

Grace married him, anyhow. She married him in spite of his size. She also married him in spite of his looks, his butterball body, his fat legs, his wide behind, his farsightedness and high blood pressure. No, Homer wasn't a looker.

Grace was. Grace could be a Pretty Woman, Miss Hollywood, Miss Vogue or Miss Libido. She had always been a model, even in the lean days when her checks paid for Homer's spaghetti at Max's.

Hegemund, the patent leather and lace

photographer for the bigtime, happened to spot her one day at Sardi's. Something happened behind Homer's back, and that was the beginning of the end for Homer. Grace needed Hegemund. And what Grace needed Hegemund for was not Hegemund personally.

Hegemund snapped the black and whites for the Fentis Fur Company. The Fentis Fur ads are first page in Vogue, the sort of spot a gal like Grace could use for self-promotion. Pretty soon Grace was the Fentis Fur Woman. But Homer couldn't see why modeling furs for Fentis should cost a woman time and a half in Hegemund's apartment. He should have known that Grace really was posing. But Homer didn't know Hegemund, and that was why Hegemund had his right eye in a black sling for the next three weeks. (Three agency gents got ringside seats. It was a clean knockout in the first few seconds of round one.)

Homer didn't understand it, but the stink in the papers did his wife plenty of good. Nicky English (*Nicky's New York*) spilled the black eye saga and made her a mystery woman. The divorce was featured in all the tabloids. People turned around and just stared and stared at poor Grace. Did Grace resent it? Why do women wear hats with feathers on them? Grace was stared at in the Waldorf, The Stork, 21, 31, The Flying Ginch and all the lesser hot spots where experienced starers ply their trade. She made the top-flight modelling jobs overnight. She was café society. There was talk of Hollywood, and from then on her photogenic puss popped into print whenever a magazine rolled off the presses.

And Homer? He didn't really want to divorce her. That was why he became the Harpo Marx among writers. Homer turned dapper. Homer dropped from 278 to 215. Homer's heart was broken. He wore it on his sleeve, as the saying goes. He cooed at every passing wench. But he still mooed over Grace.

The train jerked to a stop. I skipped out and bought a *Times* before Homer had downed his next hooker.

We found the item on page five, well screened by corsets and shoes.

FAMOUS ILLUSTRATOR
IS SUICIDE AT WEEKEND
PARTY IN WOODSTOCK

Hugo Shipley, noted illustrator, killed himself last night during the last few hours of a weekend party for a group of his friends. The guests had gone to their rooms when the sound of a shot was heard from downstairs. Shipley had locked himself into his studio. Among the guests were Nicky English, famous columnist of *The Daily Star*; Stanley Nevin, a friend; Bruce Cunningham, of The Darton Sarton, Martin and Dibble Advertising Co.; Douglas Trum, cigarette magnate; Mike Gavano, notorious East Side racketeer; and Grace Lawrence, famous model.

Shipley had for years held his place among the first-rank illustrators in the country, and his earnings had never fallen under the big brackets. He achieved wide notoriety for his fabulous weekend parties, where it was not uncommon for him to have royalty as his guests.

His career began . . .

But Homer had read enough.

'A jolly little crew,' he muttered. 'I can well understand why Shipley invited little Homer there.'

I kept my mouth shut, because I suspected what might be coming.

'Oh, well,' he sighed. 'I can't blame her for wanting to become Mrs. Trum number six. Trum's salty with lucre.'

I leaned on my elbow and fell asleep.

★   ★   ★

Homer smacked me awake in the cab, and pointed through the rear window.

'We're being tailed,' he said, chuckling.

'You're drunk,' I gurgled. 'Who in hell would tail us?'

'Two apelike gentlemen I spotted in the station. I have an uncanny instinct about that sort of thing. I have an idea they have a mission, sonny.'

Homer wasn't fooling. He signaled the cabby to stop about two blocks before his apartment. I caught a glimpse of the other cab, swinging to the curb about three blocks away. Two men hopped out.

'Come,' said Homer, bracing me at the elbow.

We jitterbugged down the street, like two stumblebums. Homer jerked me to a standstill before a store window. We pretended to window shop. The two gents on the next block stopped to chat under a lamp post.

'That's enough for me,' said Homer, guiding me briskly to the door. He paused for another instant to fumble with his little black book and stare up at the house number. Our two friends ducked into a convenient doorway. We skipped inside and nabbed an elevator.

Shtunk Smith was waiting. 'Geez,' said he. 'I am happy you have come. I am slowly going nuts, Mr. Bull. Last Friday — '

'Now,' said Homer, after his stogie was lit, 'tell me what's happened, Shtunk. Don't stutter — don't rush. I'd like to know what's gone on since I left my little ivory tower in your lily white hands.'

'Geez,' Shtunk said again. 'It is away beyond me, I am sure. I am admitting that I took a few snifters too much. Friday, it was.'

'Friday what was?'

'I am up fairly early on Friday, see? It is eleven in the a.m. I go downstairs, like always, and right away, something is happening. I find a gink poking around in our mailbox, see?'

Homer leaned forward. 'You caught him?'

'I do not catch him. He is plenty frightened when he perceives me. He runs. I run after him. He runs too fast. I make a resolve to lay off hard liquor.'

'Did he get the mail?'

The Shtunk grinned with pride. 'He gets nothing but the air. I have stopped him in the nick of time, see? I open the box and carry the mail upstairs. Then I am putting on my thinking cap.'

'Bravo!' said Homer.

'I am thinking like this,' said the Shtunk. 'I am thinking, what would Mr. Bull do if he was me? It comes to me in a flash. I decide I will stay home on account of some item in that mailbox is maybe worth a trip to the pen. You follow me?'

Homer nodded. 'So far, so noble.'

'It is here the trouble starts.' The

Shtunk lowered his eyes. 'I decide I am hungry, which I am. I phone the delicatessen for some grub. Then I decide that I am also thirsty. Likewise, I phone McKibbon's Bar for a few bottles of you-know-what. I wait until the food comes. I eat. I have a snifter with my grub, of course.'

'Of course,' I chirped.

'Of course,' said Homer.

The Shtunk fidgeted. 'After grub, I do the dishes. I also have a bottle in the kitchen on account of I do not like to massage the dishes. It helps. I come back in the studio and see the mail. I examine it. I see one letter from a bank. I see a postcard from your sister. I see another letter from this Shipley guy. Right then I decide what to do.' He paused to light a cigarette. 'I decide it is smart if I am to hide this Shipley letter, on account of because the other two is null and void.'

'Geez!' I yapped. 'All that thinking come out of you, Shtunk?'

The Shtunk frowned. 'You will please button your lip, MacAndrew!' He turned to Homer. 'I take the Shipley letter and hide it. I do a good job. Then I feel like my conscience is clear. I settle down to finish that bottle of Scotch. I work at that bottle all night, but I win out.'

'And the next day?' I asked.

'The next day, in the afternoon, I am up again,' said the Shtunk. 'And right here is the first phone call coming in.'

'That was Saturday afternoon?'

'That is correct. The phone is waking me up. I yap: 'Hello?' Some gent asks me if I am Homer Bull. I say: 'No. He will be back presently.' Then I call the delicatessen again, on account of I am hungry. The same business again happens, mostly because I am going nuts from listening to the radio. By ten o'clock I am once more in bed and also the second bottle of Scotch is gone.'

'It is Sunday afternoon when you get up?' Homer smiled.

'It is Sunday night. The phone has done it again. Again some mutt asks for Homer Bull. He is no gent this time. He hangs up on me right away.' The Shtunk reddened. 'Here is the spot where I begin to go nuts. I decide that maybe I should read this Shipley letter on account of it might be important. I search high and low. It is gone.'

'You lost it?' Homer snapped

The Shtunk was hurt.

'I do not lose it. I misplace it, see? I have forgot where I slipped it. All Sunday night I search for that damn letter. It is one in the morning when I find it. I have put it in the icebox, with ice cubes. I forget it because I never use the cubes for Scotch, see? I read it. It sounds important. Then I go nuts trying to find your address. This I have really lost. I cannot send you a wire, until I call Queens Features, where I get the name of your dump in Virginia.' He paused. 'That is all which happens until this morning in the a.m. Seven o'clock the phone is ringing. I am plenty mad on account of it has woke me up so early. It rings again at eight. Seven times it rings. It is always the same voice which is asking me the same question and then hanging up on me.'

Homer's little black book was out. 'When was the last call?'

'I am saving this last phone call for the

topper,' grinned the Shtunk. 'The last call is happening only twenty minutes ago. It is the same gink, but this time I do not wait for him to talk. I am ready for him, see? Before he can open his yap, I say: 'Go to hell, you crud!' I hear the gink begin to curse. I hang up then. I guess that wise apple will not bother you anymore, Mr. Bull.'

The Shtunk guessed wrong. The phone rang. Homer's expression didn't change. The Shtunk leaped for the phone. 'You want I should tell that gink off again?'

'Hold on,' said Homer. 'I'll speak to the gentleman.'

He lifted the telephone and said: 'Yes, this is Mr. Homer Bull . . . What . . . ? Oh, that's silly; I like Woodstock . . . You're wrong, sonny. I'd recommend you getting a morning paper.' He dropped the phone and beamed. 'I am afraid most gangsters read nothing but the sports section, Hank. It's no wonder they're maladjusted.'

He opened the cupboard and poured a tall one for the Shtunk. Then he poured a short one for himself. I reached for the bottle, but he whisked it away. 'No more for you, sonny. You've got a responsible job to do. You'll be driving us to Woodstock in a few minutes.'

He spread the *Times* on the table.

'That'll be your last drink this week, Shtunk,' he said, fixing the little man with a baleful eye. 'I have a little job for you.'

He cut the Shipley item out of the paper and handed it to the Shtunk.

'I want some information, you understand? I want all you can get on these four characters: Stanley Nevin, Bruce Cunningham, Douglas Trum and Mike Gavano.'

The Shtunk whistled, 'Mike Gavano!'

'Familiar with the name?'

The Shtunk whistled again. A higher note. 'Some of my best friends have been bumped off by that guy!'

'You know him?'

'I am lucky. I do not know him. I do not want to know him.' He scratched his head. 'It will not be very easy to get a line on that gent. People who gab about Mike are not what you would call a common occurrence, on account of all of them that has opened their yaps about him already are pushing up the daisies.'

Homer said: 'Do your best. Cunning-ham and Trum will be easy, I'm sure. You can pay a visit to my friend Gurney, the editor of the *Star*. Gurney will give you the key to their morgue.'

The Shtunk squirmed. 'This I am not used to doing. It is not very cosy mixing with the stiffs.'

'Don't be a sap,' I said. 'A *newspaper* morgue is where they keep clippings and pictures of celebrities. The only stiffs you'll see will be the zombie reporters. They're the living dead.'

Homer toyed with Shipley's note, then handed it to me. It was typewritten haphazardly, in the manner of a hunt-and-peck stenographer.

The invitation read:

Be quick, Homer!
    I almost forgot that you specialize in comic strip characters.
    You'll find plenty up here this week-end. Please come up Friday.

Shipley

'Droll,' I said. 'But does it mean anything?'

Homer shrugged and stuffed the note away. 'We'll see.'

He turned to the Shtunk and the news clipping. 'I've never heard of Stanley Nevin — an ordinary mortal, no doubt, probably just a friend of Shipley's. Get me as much on Nevin as you can — where he lives, what he does, who he sleeps with. Phone me at Woodstock as soon as you've got anything worth mentioning. I'll expect your call sometime tonight.'

The Shtunk gulped his Scotch and went.

Homer sent me packing. 'Put enough of our needs in one suitcase, Hank. I don't think we'll be up there very long.'

'I don't get it,' I groused. 'What's so urgent? After all, Shipley's a suicide — he won't make a very entertaining host.'

'I'll bet on Shipley,' mused Homer. 'Dead or alive. After all, he was the world's best party boy, Hank. I like his guest list. It seems to me that we may find something up there — something worth putting into a story. We'll be doing a job, you see.'

'Wishful thinking,' said I.

'And besides,' Homer rumbled on, 'I'm like the kid and the jar of jelly. Tell me I can't reach it and I'll break my back getting it. Somebody doesn't want me up there, Hank. Why? I feel the need for a post-mortem vacation. Somebody doesn't want me to vacation at Woodstock. It has all the elements of something or other.'

'Malarkey!'

I went into the bedroom and packed. After all, how could I expect Homer to admit that he was visiting Woodstock for a gander at Grace?

Love is like that.

3

Think, Swink, Think

I drove. Homer maintained a moody silence until we crossed the Washington Bridge.

'It becomes increasingly difficult to believe that Hugo Shipley committed suicide,' he muttered, as though he were debating with the Palisades. 'I knew him casually. In our few chance meetings, he impressed me as being a man who might have been a cad, an egomaniac, a poseur, a Casanova of the Hollywood School of Seduction. But a suicide? I wonder.'

'Not dramatic enough for Hugo,' I snorted. 'He'd rather be found dead than a suicide.'

Kingston lay behind us, and we entered the tortuous two-lane road that dipped and wound around the snowy hills. Ah there, Woodstock! Sudden memories clouded my brain. This, in a way, was my native land. Not too long ago, when art meant more to me than comic strips, I had tested my brush in these ruddy valleys, fiddling with light and shade and a business called chiaroscuro.

Woodstock? Woodstock is Woodstock. A cluster of small stores on the main street, a small gallery, and wooden restaurants warmed with candlelight and the never-ending buzz of chatter. An inn, two inns, three inns. You could eat in several languages in Woodstock and then belch in the colloquial without any regrets. This was a town of free souls, of artists and writers, models and morons — a town to quiet the soul, or make it live again.

Homer nudged me into the present.

'Pick up this chap,' he said. 'He looks cold.'

I stopped the car alongside the lone figure plodding up the road. Homer swung open the door.

'Want a lift?'

The man in the black overcoat turned his head and showed us a row of gold teeth set in an ugly mouth. His rat eyes darted from Homer to me. He was making up his mind.

'Yeah, sure,' he said, and got in. 'Damn cold up here. How far you going?'

'As far as you go,' Homer said, turning in his seat to face the man. 'You're bound for Shipley's place, aren't you, Mr. Gavano?'

The man was surprised. He raised his beetle brows and said: 'I'll be damned! You ain't — '

'Oh, but I am,' said Homer, grinning impishly. 'You didn't expect me, did you? My name's Homer Bull.'

Gavano reset his face. 'Expect you? Nuts. I ain't expecting nobody. Why should I be expecting anybody?'

'I thought Shipley might have told you I'd be up. You see, I'm late. Business prevented me from coming up on Friday night. But had I known — ' Here he paused to beam at Gavano. ' — had I but known that you'd be here, Mike — wild horses couldn't have kept me away.'

'A funny man, eh?'

Homer went on. 'It must be getting rather stuffy up at Shipley's place since he — ah, committed suicide.'

Gavano was silent.

I swung the car into a sharp right turn, and we began to skid and climb up into the hills.

Homer nudged me again. 'Another wanderer,' he said, and pointed ahead. 'Shall we stop for the lady, Hank?'

I stopped. It was Eileen Tucker.

'Why, it's Hank.' She smiled. 'Whatever in the world are you doing up here?'

I introduced Homer, and held open the rear door.

Eileen's smile faded suddenly. I thought I saw fear in her eyes. She closed the door. 'Oh, no, thanks,' she said. 'I'd rather walk — really. I'll see you later. Wait for me at the house.'

I didn't insist.

Homer said: 'Do you always frighten little women, Gavano?'

'Nuts!' said Gavano.

Homer shrugged. 'A brilliant conversationalist.'

We passed through the gate on the border of Shipley's huge slice of acreage. Once, on a hike with Shirley, I had seen the squat, sprawling estate that was the home of Hugo Shipley. Shirley and I had played guessing games for hours. What could a lone man want with so much house? Even a seasoned rake didn't need eight bedrooms. (We counted the windows on the second floor.)

Shipley was known internationally, of course, for his parties — his dizzy society-column brawls that started every Thursday night and ended in confusion. But after the parties — what? We pictured the great illustrator, clad in his overpublicized pajamas, stalking the great halls, or eating his curds and whey in the monstrous raftered room that was his dining nook.

Shipley made his million in the days when illustrating for the big weeklies paid better dividends than Bethlehem Steel. His style never changed, nor did his vogue pass. He had a happy facility for pleasing editors, if not by his gloomy black and whites, then by his full color illustrated orgies in the hills.

Tall, dark and handsome as a Mephisto, he had lived a life brimming over with fair-weather friends and bitter enemies. He was a boon to gossip columnists, caterers and tabloid readers. He had lived hard.

I laughed at the idea of Hugo Shipley committing suicide.

I swung the car through the second gate and down the road to Nat Tucker's nest, where Nat waved me to a stop. I introduced Homer. Gavano walked away up the driveway without a word.

'Peculiar cuss,' whispered Nat, jerking his thumb Gavano's way. 'Just like one of them gangster fellers you see in the movies.'

'Another reason for avoiding the movies,' I said.

Nat led us inside. There was a fire in the hearth and a drink in the cupboard for each of us. Homer spread himself in a rocker and his eyes wandered around the room.

'A cosy little place you have here, Tucker,' he said. 'Been living here long?'

'Five years this Christmas. Been here ever since Mr. Shipley bought the estate. He's made it awful pleasant for us here.'

'It agrees with Eileen,' I said. 'We just met her down the road, and she's prettier than ever.'

Tucker glowed. 'Eileen's just finished

her schooling down in Kingston. She's learned typing, you know. Mr. Shipley used her now and then as a typist. Paid her good, too.'

'Typing?' asked Homer. 'Shipley was turning to fiction, then?'

'I guess you'd call it that. Some business about a book of memoirs, it was.' Nat shook his head gloomily. 'It's a sad business up there. Never thought Mr. Shipley would take his own life.'

'How many others did Shipley employ around the place?'

'Two.'

That was a surprise, even to Homer. 'Two others in help? How in the world could two people manage that big house?'

Nat scratched his head. 'I couldn't rightly say, 'cause I never did inquire. But I do know that Mr. Shipley didn't like many servants around him. Said they got in his hair.'

'But how in hell could he run those — ?'

'The parties?' Nat smiled. 'O' course, he'd have many more in help for one of his shindigs, but they were mostly waiters and such from town.'

'Odd,' said Homer. 'The two, I suppose, are a housekeeper and a valet?'

Tucker laughed. 'Mr. Shipley didn't fancy a valet. He had a cook — that's Minnie Minton. And Minnie's husband, Lester — well, I guess you might call him a butler, at that.'

'Butler and housemaid?' I suggested.

'Well, he must be a housemaid, Hank. Minnie Minton, now, she just cooks. I don't imagine Minnie does anything else but cook. Mebbe after you meet Lester, you'll understand who makes the beds and keeps the place clean. Lester's a queer one.' And he rolled his eyes toward the ceiling.

We left the car at Nat's, at his suggestion. The main garage, he told us, was full up.

The wizened Yankee who admitted us was surly. 'Now we don't want any more reporters,' he snapped. 'There ain't a thing to get up here. The guests won't talk and there's nothing to snap with your cameras.'

Homer introduced himself, and the

man's tone changed.

'Homer Bull, did you say? Well, now, that's different.' He pumped Homer's hand. 'I'm Jesse Swink — sheriff. Follow your funny page stuff every day. Damned good — and clever, too. But what's up here to interest you, eh, Bull?'

Homer mentioned Shipley's invitation. 'I've wanted, too, to study your country routine, Mr. Swink. I'm planning a farm story, you see. Might even use you as the sheriff in the case. That is, if you don't mind.'

Swink softened even more and led us into the library. Homer wooed him further with a cigar.

'Are you planning an inquest?' asked Homer.

Swink pulled at his mustache nervously. 'Matter of fact, no. Lem Bruck — he's the coroner — called it open-and-shut suicide. But I don't know *what* it is.'

I caught a broad wink from Homer. 'You have your doubts?'

'Noooo.' Swink half shut his eyes. 'I'd call it a hunch, Bull. Just a hunch.'

'What sort of a hunch?'

Swink paused, making faces at the ceiling. 'I can't say.' He turned to Homer suddenly. 'Ever get a strong feeling about somethin' without knowing why?'

'Often. That sort of hunch might be worth working on.'

'Can't *understand* it.' Swink's arms went out stiffly; his eyebrows shot up. 'It ain't the way the man died. Shipley died like a suicide, all right.'

'But?'

Swink set his hat back on his bald head. 'Can't find me a reason in the world, Bull. Except — ' He suddenly sat down, 'that these people — these guests of his — make me leery. They just make me *leery*, is all!'

'You don't like them?'

'Hell,' said Swink, 'that ain't it. Ain't it at all. It's just that they're — well, they're *queer*, is all. Never saw such an odd bunch in all my days. Good friend o' theirs dies — *good friend*, mind you. And — and nobody seems sorry. Nobody's mourning! See what I mean?'

'I think so,' said Homer, puffing slowly.

Swink wrestled with his jacket pocket

and brought out a sheet of notepaper. 'They're all on this sheet. Mebbe you know some of 'em, Bull?'

I squinted at the list over Homer's shoulder.

Minnie Minton — Shipley's cook
Lester Minton — butler
Grace Lawrence — model
Bruce Cunningham — advertising man
Nick English — newspaper man
Olympe Deming — secretary
Stanley Nevin — friend
Douglas Trum — cigarette man
Mike Gavano — friend

Homer said: 'I know only Miss Lawrence. She used to be my wife.'

Swink's jaw dropped. 'Well, now, that's interesting, ain't it now?'

Homer didn't say. 'I've heard of Nicky English, of course. Most New Yorkers would know his name — he's quite a famous columnist. They're all still here, Swink?'

'Yep, I told 'em to stay. Felt I ought to talk this thing over with Bruck this afternoon. Couldn't get myself to let 'em go, somehow. Funny, ain't it? Me holdin' 'em here and not knowin' why, I mean. Heaven knows what I thought I'd find, diggin' around this house today.'

'I'm glad you held them here,' said Homer, rising. 'Mind if I take a look around? I'd like to see his studio first.'

Swink led us through the awesome beamed dining room and from there through a small hallway to the studio.

Shipley had built his workroom on the north side of the house. It was a huge affair, forming a wing with three exposures and only one door. The door itself leaned crazily against the wall, more or less held upright by the lower hinge which had not broken away after a terrific impact.

Three walls of the room were really walls of windows, skillfully designed to give modern light and yet not disturb the rococo theme of the studio itself. For rococo the studio certainly was. Shipley must have understood his audience. He had created this room, obviously, to satisfy his guests, his editors and all their press agents.

I examined the handsomely carved oak easel and remembered my first sight of Hugo Shipley leering prettily into the camera, in a publicity picture for a women's magazine. He had surrounded himself with the sort of garbage even a French court painter wouldn't have chosen, it was that bad. Pure corn, from the heavy English rafters to the theatre lobby drapes that completely covered the only un-windowed wall.

Pure corn, sure — but the effect of the room as a unit made me step lightly on the deep rugs, and even look for an ashtray for my dwindling butt. I was impressed, in spite of my distaste. Or maybe it was the crimson stain on the white rug Homer was examining that made my heart pound off beat.

'There's where he was lying,' Swink said, and dropped to his knees to demonstrate. 'Like this. His head facing them windows. The gun right here — not over a foot from his right hand.'

Homer joined Swink on the floor. He crawled around the huge bloodstain slowly, his fat tail jellying gently. He paused finally, to sit cross-legged on the rug and open his little book. He turned to Swink.

'Powder burns?'

Swink nodded briskly. 'Plenty. Couldn't have held that gun more than six inches away from his heart. He was a mess, Bull.'

Homer rose to examine the door.

Swink said: 'The door wasn't in that position, o' course, when I got here. I pushed it back against the wall so's it'd be out o' the way. It was hangin' by that bottom hinge.'

Homer fiddled with the key. 'You found this key in the door?'

'Yep. Shipley locked himself in and left the key just the way you see it. Made it impossible to unlock the door from the outside.'

'Then somebody had another key?'

'Yep. Shipley's secretary, Miss Deming.' Swink reached into his pants and showed the key. 'Only other key to the door there is.' He demonstrated how the inside key had jammed the lock.

'Let me get this straight,' said Homer. 'Miss Deming, then, had the key with her at the time she heard the shot?'

'No, she didn't. The key was up in her room, she says. Says she heard the shot when she was in the library. She ran to the door, scared stiff. The butler came next. In the excitement, she forgot all about her key. The butler broke down the door.'

There was a pause while Homer scrawled the item in his book. Then he stepped through the door into the hallway and stood there, staring into the studio. His eyes were fixed upon the stain of blood near the window. Finally he began to walk backwards slowly, until he stood in the gloom of the dining room. There he remained, while Swink scratched his head, squinted at me confusedly, and blew through his mustache.

Homer returned. 'Was there any light in the studio when the body was discovered?'

'I'll be damned!' said Swink. 'Never thought o' that question. Never asked.'

'Just a straw,' Homer said. 'I'm not sure it means anything.'

Swink walked at Homer's heels while

he toured the room.

'Strange place,' murmured Homer. 'Damnedest studio I ever did see.' He faced the easel, arms akimbo. 'Look here, Hank. This easel backs up on the north light. Why do artists insist on north light, if not to make use of it?'

He was right. The massive easel stood with its back to the north window.

'Hell, Shipley wasn't a longhair,' I explained. 'He didn't really need that light.'

'So?'

'He might have been working at night the last time he used the easel,' I added, and pointed to the fancy lighting contraption to the left of it. 'He might have been using this gadget.'

Swink said: 'You think of the dangdest things, Bull.'

'Only straws, Swink. Only straws.' He fingered his jowls. 'You don't suppose the easel could have been moved, eh, Swink?'

'It *weren't* moved!' snapped Swink. 'No solitary thing in this room was moved, unless Shipley fixed it that way before he died.'

'You've had someone in this room since then?'

Swink was flustered. 'Well, no. But I noticed the danged thing when I came in the room. It sat just the way you see it.'

Homer lifted the easel and peered at the rug. 'You're probably right.' He rubbed the oak frame and fiddled with the palette, scraping with his fingernail. I saw him pocket a few tubes of paint before he turned away and crossed the room to the wall of drapes.

I fingered the stuff. 'Crepe de chine, Homer?'

'Figured monk's cloth,' he corrected, holding the material up to the light. 'Rather novel, don't you think, covering the whole wall with it?'

'Ducky! A decorator's dream. At ten-cents-a-foot profit, some pantywaist must have bought himself a seat in the yard goods industry.'

Swink was bored. 'What do you think, Bull?'

Homer sank heavily into a chair and played with his jaw. 'I think we should have an inquest.'

The country dick was excited at the idea. 'Then you've got a hunch, too? You think you have something?'

'I don't know — I'm only guessing. But if you can arrange to have your inquest on Wednesday afternoon, I have an idea that it will prove — ah — worth our while, Swink.'

Swink paced the floor. I caught a quick wink from Homer. Swink turned on his heel suddenly.

'I'll call Bruck right away!'

'Good!' said Homer, and got up. He walked through the door whistling through his teeth, as happy as a lark.

4

Grace Knows from Nothing

Homer's severest critics (in the Brooklyn Police Department) would always say: 'Homer Bull? That butterball! He takes his time — and everybody else's!'

But Wilkinson, the man who mattered, would add: 'So what, you plugs? Ain't I always told you slow and steady wins the race?'

Which meant that Wilkinson thought Homer slow, but steady. It also meant that Wilkinson approved of Homer's methods and always appreciated his results. He would walk into the flat loaded down with pictures, files and fingerprints, and wait with his cigar while Homer sighed and fussed and inevitably emerged from the debris with a good idea. But slowly. Homer always took his clues as they came. Even when confronted with witnesses, suspects, stools, or

43

gunmen, the system remained the same. Homer allowed them the calm of a drink or a good cigar. Homer came late, but he stayed long. No fuss, no bother, no rub-in — and never a third degree.

We were alone in the library. Homer relaxed. He had returned from Grace's room bright-eyed and eager, just as though she might have given him an important shred of evidence, or a hint, or something else, maybe. You never could tell, with Homer. We had then wandered through half of the house, like weekend guests on the loose. We gawked at the collection of French impressionists in the main hall, admired the view from the broad windows in the living room, and even paused for a one-sided billiard fracas in the pine-paneled game room.

Now he toyed with a volume of the collected works of Shipley, a gaudy scrap book as big as a table top, while I dug deep into a choice bit of pornography, illustrated by a madman. (I made a mental note to take this tidbit away with me. Kleptomania runs in my family.)

'Shipley's later illustrations seem to

have suffered a change,' said Homer brightly. 'And when I say suffered, I mean improved.'

I dropped the pornography grudgingly and looked over his shoulder. 'You've got a keen eye, Sherlock — his style *has* changed. He must have been really trying to draw a bit in his last moments.'

I hardly noticed Swink and Nevin walk in. When I looked up from the meaty tome, Homer had already said hello, and nodded me into the group.

'That's fruity stuff, eh?' said Nevin.

'Very bad art,' I said. 'It smells of high-school washrooms.'

'You've picked up the worst in Hugo's collection,' Nevin said. 'I'd recommend the *Heinrich Kley*. At least Kley could draw that sort of tripe.'

Homer arranged the party in his corner, leaving me to the book if the going got boresome. I looked over the edge of the cover at Nevin.

He seemed tired. He was a handsome guy, indeed, in a dark blue ski suit, skillfully designed to promote his broad shoulders and conceal the slight droop in them. He had an odd face — the face of a college boy who has only aged around the eyes. The face was cherubic, photogenic. But the eyes were very tired. His features had the baffling simplicity of the guy you always think you know in the subway. He looked at you out of the past. You knew him from somewhere, somehow. His eyes had the tired, simple stare of an overworked clothing model, or an overworked law clerk, or the good-looking guy your sister used to go with.

Swink said: 'Mr. Nevin's just been out skiing.' (He mouthed it as though he meant: 'Here's the first one. See what you can do with him.')

'Just up to the big hill,' said Nevin. 'Thought I'd like to sketch that big old oak.'

'You do artwork?' I asked. 'Let's see what you got.'

'Oh, I'm no artist,' he said. 'Just fiddle a bit with a pencil. I couldn't even get started today — too cold.'

'I suppose Shipley's marked a few trails on this hill of his?' Homer asked.

'Three of them,' said Nevin. 'And all

46

excellent. But poor Hugo never lived to really enjoy them — this was the first year the trails were usable.'

'A pity. Shipley must have been an expert at the sport, from all the reports I've read.'

'He was unbeatable.'

Homer squinted at the end of his cigar for a long time and said nothing. I remembered the trick. Homer really disliked asking questions — annoying people — with pot shots. It was always much easier, he said, to annoy them with silence. He was trying to force the next few words from Nevin. He wanted Nevin to say something, anything, unquestioned.

But the deadly quiet didn't break. Nevin leaned on his elbows and stared at the rug. The trick had failed.

'Know Shipley long?' Homer asked finally.

'For about five years.'

'Through business?'

'No, we were good friends.' I thought I heard his voice tremble on the last word. He kept staring down at his legs. 'I met

Hugo in his penthouse — when he had one on Madison Avenue.' He spoke slowly, almost measuring his words, like a high-school orator making rebuttal.'

'At one of his famous parties?'

Nevin looked up at Homer. 'Yes, it was at a party. He told me he might use me for one of his illustrations. That was how I got to know him, you see. We've been close friends ever since.'

Suddenly I understood how I came to know this man. I had seen his face over and over again in Shipley's illustrations. Nevin's handsome pan had appeared in every national magazine that featured Shipley. It must have certainly hit Homer the same way, I knew, and wondered what he would do with the thought.

'Ever up here before?' Homer asked.

There was a pause.

'Once or twice.'

'How long ago was that?'

'A few years ago — maybe three.'

'Now, that's odd,' said Homer honestly. 'You say you were good friends, and yet you rarely visited him here. How come?'

Nevin seemed annoyed with that one. 'I

— Hugo knew that I didn't care for his parties, nor his so-called friends.'

'I see,' Homer almost apologized. 'Then you met him in town, usually?'

'Yes. We saw each other almost every time Hugo came to town.'

Homer studied his cigar, and I felt another spell of quiet coming on. But this time the trick worked.

Nevin said: 'I think Hugo understood and appreciated my attitude about his — his friends.'

'I don't understand,' said Homer. 'You mean that Shipley knew that a lot of his friends were phoney?'

Nevin smiled wryly. 'Indeed he did. As a matter of fact, Hugo had started a book about them.'

'You're not serious?' Homer feigned surprise.

'Oh yes. Hugo thought his friends interesting enough for publication. Too bad he died — I think he would have had a bestseller.'

'He had a sense of humor, didn't he?'

'Hugo wasn't kidding in that book, from what he told me.' Nevin rose.

Homer said: 'I think you can help me, Nevin. I'm curious about this last weekend party, especially since I was invited. Do you think Shipley intended to invite only those people who would annoy each other? Sort of a gathering of cross-purposes?'

Nevin thought a moment. 'I couldn't say. I wasn't invited — just dropped by. You see, these people are all strangers to me.'

'Even so, would you say that Shipley might invite such a mixed group up here with that idea in mind? Sort of a gag?'

'Possibly.' Nevin started for the door.

Swink said: 'By the way, Mr. Nevin, I just spoke to the coroner. He says there'll be an inquest on Wednesday afternoon.'

Nevin was deadpan. 'Does that mean we must stay in the house?'

'I'd prefer it.'

'Very well. I'll see you later. Got to take off these ski togs.'

When Nevin had gone, Swink asked anxiously: 'What do you make of that bird?'

Homer chuckled. 'Make of him? I make

nothing of him. Old friend of Shipley's — a bit broken up by his death.'

'Seems like a nice guy,' I added. 'Can't blame him for hating the lice Shipley called his friends.'

'Did you meet any of the others?' Swink asked.

'I visited with Miss Lawrence. A very charming piece. My ex-wife, you know.'

Swink said: 'Unh? Well, I'd better tell the others about the inquest.'

Homer waited until Swink had gone before allowing himself a whinny. 'That old scallion'll be changing his pants from sheer excitement, or I miss my guess.'

'He and I both. What's cooking?'

'I visited with the Mintons after Grace. A very funny couple. *Superman*. A little on the moronic side. Says he and his wife heard Lester — and he *does* do the beds — would make a swell antagonist for the shot from the kitchen — it's only a dozen yards away. Lester found Miss Deming wailing at the door. Lester then proceeded to force the door. He says it was easy — it would be, for Lester. When the door was opened, Miss Deming fainted.

Then Mrs. Minton joined her in a sympathetic faint.'

'Must be an ox. I thought that door looked pretty solid.'

'Not an ox — an ape. Lester is a reformed monster — about sixty-two, with football shoulders and a torso like Gargantua.'

'You should know.'

Homer grinned. 'And that brings us to Grace. She's well heeled. Gone high hat.' He closed his eyes. 'But still — ah — charming.'

'I suppose you gave her the business? I mean with questions?'

'Her story fits. I mean to say that if we find confusion here, little Gracie had no stake in it. Her job is hooking Trum — even though she doesn't seem to have her heart in her work.'

'Neat,' I teased. 'Detective eliminates ex-wife from gruesome slaying!'

'Nonsense,' he said to his cigar. 'Detective does nothing of the sort. But how does cockeyed cartoonist deduce the man murdered?'

'You asked for an inquest.'

'You're thinking wishfully, sonny.'

'Nuts! Why not allow the characters to go home, then?'

'I can dream, can't I?' Homer smiled slyly.

'Not with *our* deadline coming up,' I snapped.

'Touché!' said Homer. 'You're beginning to think like a lending-library detective. You're maturing, Hank. Pretty soon you'll stop talking in gag-line patois, and then I'll be bringing the clues to you.'

'Stop salving me, Homer. Have you got anything?'

'I'm not quite sure,' he said seriously. 'The threads are beginning to unravel in this thing. They may lead us somewhere. They may lead us behind the eight ball.'

I groaned. 'Double talk! You mean you haven't any ideas — even silly ideas? What about Gavano? Did Grace drop any hints? Do you think it's murder, really?'

'One thing at a time!' Homer closed his eyes and made a little face. 'I haven't got a thing on Gavano, Watson. And all I could get from Grace — ah — didn't amount to much. She reports that she walked into the studio after Lester and his wife and Olympe Deming were there. She was number four.' He got up and tapped me on the chest. 'You see, there isn't much, so far.'

I saw. He was throwing me crumbs — giving me things to think about. He was offering me the facts and retaining his conclusions. Oh, well, maybe Homer had only come up for the chance to be around Grace. Love is a business I get only from comic strips. Was that love-light agleam in Homer's baby blue eyes? Could be. But I could imagine a man looking that way after his second shot of rye. Or a winner at Jamaica. Could it be that Homer was going love-punchy?

'I don't suppose Grace could tell you much about the others?' I let sarcasm creep into my questions.

'How could she?' Homer sighed. 'The little dove has eyes for nobody but Trum.'

'She must have changed.'

'Not at all. A little broader in the beam, perhaps, but otherwise she's the same old Gracie. A gal with a purpose.'

'Trum must be a prize package.'

'Trum is. He has a corner in the cigarette mart. His cash register tinkles every time we take a drag, Hank. He's well salted, all right, but he's got a past as black as Mussolini's shirt. Five wives.' He held up a pudgy hand. 'Can't you just see our Gracie as the sixth Mrs. Trum?'

'I can't see Gracie nohow.'

'You are a man of violent dislikes, sonny.' Homer chuckled. 'It doesn't become a detective to dislike so thoroughly. We must take our evidence where we find it and reserve all judgments for the last chapter.'

'Should I apologize?' I asked.

'For disliking Gracie?' He actually laughed out loud. 'Fiddlesticks! You and I are in perfect agreement there. But we mustn't be too hard on the lady, sonny. She has her good points, even though they can only be appreciated by an ex-husband.'

'You've hit the *frail* right on the head,' I gagged.

Homer joined me in the ensuing laughter.

5

Homer Plays Professor Quiz

We were gulping Minnie Minton's coffee and munching her scones when Swink minced in.

'They're all in the living room, Bull,' he said. 'Are you ready to go?'

'Go where?' He frowned.

'Inside,' said Swink blankly. 'To question 'em.'

Homer was caught between dunks. 'I can't see any reason for gathering them in one room and going through an imitation inquest. What have you told them?'

Swink explained that he had told them it was to be an examination before the inquest.

'Is that legal?'

'Nothing illegal about it. Got Eileen Tucker to take it all down in shorthand. I don't see why you — '

'I suppose it's all right. I just didn't like

the idea of facing an audience, I guess. Let's go.'

I counted eleven of them in the living room, including Minnie Minton, who sat playing with her apron in the corner. Homer told them that there would be a few questions, opened his little book and rubbed his nose. A little guy in an Esquirish jacket jumped up to shake Homer's hand.

'If this isn't terrific,' he snapped. 'Queen Features covers the Shipley suicide. You're Homer Bull, aren't you?'

Homer nodded and shook his hand. 'Nicky English?'

'The same. What in hell brings you here, Bull?' He eyed Homer narrowly and his thin lips curled.

'I'm a guest, Nicky. A little late, but not too late for the fun, eh?'

'You oughta know,' he leered. 'Maybe I can't see the comic strip angle.' He shrugged and sat down.

Nicky was nasty. But Nicky was smart. He had to be. I knew him only from the little photo slug over his column in the *Daily Star*. Rumor, gossip and slander were also meat to the millions of readers who ferreted in his column for the insidious malignancies he knew how to dish out. Nicky's column. *Nicky's New York*, was syndicated to over four hundred newspapers daily, including the Lithuanian.

Homer took a deep breath and said: 'It would be a help if I could review the discovery of Hugo Shipley's body. I have already spoken to Lester and Mrs. Minton.' He turned to smile at Olympe Deming. 'You were next in the room, weren't you, Miss Deming?'

I caught her nod and pulled out my pencil to sketch the characters, reading from left to right around the room. That was why Eileen was first on my sketch pad. I fumbled with Eileen. She was too pretty. You can't do much with even features — not if you're a cartoonist. I couldn't make Eileen pretty enough. I missed my watercolor box; her blue eyes were that tempting. And her hair — it would have been a thrill to put that shade of brown against the smooth pink wash of her skin. (It was even more beautiful when she caught my eye and blushed a bit.) Eileen had grown into womanhood and made good at it. Eileen was sweet and lovely and trim and cute and shapely and okay.

'And who followed Miss Deming?'

Grace Lawrence said: 'I did, honey, remember?'

Homer blushed and fussed with his tie. 'Of course. He beamed. 'And then — '

'I was next,' said Nevin. 'And then Nicky English.'

After Nicky came Bruce Cunningham, followed by Trum. Gavano was the last.

Homer said: 'And we can't forget Mr. Tucker. I suppose you saw the body, Nat?'

Tucker was startled. 'I did, at that. But it was much later — 'round midnight, wasn't it, Lester?'

'After midnight,' Lester said.

'And Eileen?'

Nat answered for her. 'She was asleep. Didn't know about Shipley until this morning.'

'I see,' said Homer. 'Have you been working very long for Shipley, Eileen?'

'Not very.' She smiled. 'Since Friday morning on this last job.'

'This wasn't the first job, then?'

'Oh, no. I did some of his correspondence once in a while.'

'You did typing only?'

'I took shorthand notes and did the typing.'

Homer turned to Olympe. 'But I thought you were Shipley's secretary, Miss Deming?'

I caught a wink from Grace Lawrence. But if Homer expected to get a rise out of Olympe, he must have been disappointed.

'I *was* his secretary,' she said evenly. 'I was not his stenographer.'

There was a silence, long enough to allow Homer another light for his cigar. Olympe turned toward Grace Lawrence and stared the smile off her lips.

'Did you have any regular working hours, Eileen?'

'I had no regular hours. Mr. Shipley called me when he needed me. Most of the time, on this last job, I worked with him in the mornings. But that was unusual, for Mr. Shipley — he usually called me in rather late in the afternoon, or early in the evening, when he didn't have guests around. But he seemed to be in a hurry to get this last job finished — or rather, started. I worked with him on Friday, Saturday and Sunday morning.'

'Ever work with him at night?'

Did she color a bit?

'I was with Mr. Shipley last night for about half an hour.'

Cunningham whispered a wisecrack to Grace. It must have been funny, because the redhead covered her wide mouth with a handkerchief. Nat squirmed in his chair and glared at them.

Homer went on: 'What sort of work were you doing on this last job?'

'It was a book. Mr. Shipley referred to it as his memoirs.'

I had my eye on the crowd, waiting for a reaction to this bit of news. There was none. The business of Shipley's book must have been common knowledge to all of them.

'How much of this book had you done?'

'About a chapter, I guess. Mr. Shipley explained that there would be about ten typewritten pages to each chapter. I had done about nine pages of his dictation.'

'That's pretty slow progress, isn't it?'

'That's all he had dictated,' Eileen explained. 'He gave me quite a few pages of handwritten notes on Sunday morning — but I hadn't begun to type those.'

'Did you bring the manuscript?'

Eileen fumbled with her handkerchief.

'I haven't got it. It was stolen from the house sometime last night or this morning.'

Nat said: 'We've looked high and low for that piece of writin', Mr. Bull, but there ain't no use lookin' anymore.' He glared around the room. 'Them notes was thieved out of Eileen's desk!' Olympe jumped to her feet.

'You mean you've lost that manuscript?' she raged. 'You little fool! I told Hugo he was insane when he hired you!'

Eileen squared off with her chin. 'You misunderstand me, Miss Deming. I don't mean that I've lost the notes. I mean that they've been stolen!'

'I don't believe you!'

Eileen broke down. The shorthand pad slipped from her hands and she ran out of the room. I wanted to smack down the imitation Dietrich for abusing the poor kid. But that would have been stupid. I dropped my sketch pad on the chair and ducked into the hall to catch Eileen.

I found her in the library, stifling her sobs. She buried her head in my chest and I patted her shoulder gently and tried to act the big brother. But it was tough — Eileen didn't feel like a sister in my arms.

'Don't let that peroxide punk get you,' I soothed.

She made a funny little face and tilted her head in vexation. 'But I can't understand it. I saw that manuscript just before I went to bed last night. It was on my desk in the living room where I'd been working on it. Then this morning, when I was ready to report for work, it was gone — all of it, even the shorthand notes.'

I tried to think like a detective. 'Your dad left the house shortly after midnight. That means the house was open until he returned. What time was that?'

'Dad says he came back shortly before two.'

'Did he notice that the notes were missing then?'

Eileen couldn't say.

'That makes it simple,' I deduced. 'Most likely they were gone by the time he returned. It means that any one of these amateur crooks might have walked through your front door last night, swiped the epic, and walked back to the house as calm as you please.'

'That must be it,' said Eileen.

'That is it,' I said. I held her hands. 'Got any ideas who it might be, honey?'

'Any one of them might have done it.'

'That's what I thought.'

'No, wait,' she added. 'I can't include Grace Lawrence. Grace Lawrence was the only one who didn't seem interested in the book.'

I laughed again. 'That's a laugh. Only reason why Gracie wasn't interested is the fact that Gracie didn't know that manuscript was worth a few thousand potato chips.'

Eileen was surprised. 'Why should it be worth so much money?'

I chucked her under her chin. 'Blackmail, honey. Shipley probably knew plenty about that gang in there. But puh-lenty! Can't you see Gavano swiping the stuff and holding out for dough from a big shot like Trum? That is, if Trum was included in the dirty linen. What about Nicky English? He'd have enough fodder for that cesspool column of his to last a few years. I don't know about Cunningham, Trum or Nevin — but they all might want the manuscript just in self-defense.'

I saw the light of understanding creep into her blue eyes.

'I see,' she murmured. 'Little Eileen has been awfully naïve, Hank. The country mouse is getting smarter by the minute, thanks to you.'

It was an old approach, but her eyes told me that she didn't mind it too much. I had lots to say and a couple of stray ideas about what I'd do, but before I could drop another gem Nat Tucker popped into the room, bending over Homer as he came.

Homer said: 'Break it up, MacBarry-more; I must have a word with the lass.'

I gave Eileen her hands.

'Tell me, Eileen,' Homer began, 'do you remember any part of that manuscript?'

'I only typewrote the part that Mr. Shipley dictated,' she said.

'Then you hadn't yet reached the handwritten notes?'

'You mean did I read them? I didn't — I couldn't. You see, it was very difficult to understand his sort of handwriting — queerest writing I ever saw.'

'Illegible?'

'The handwriting wasn't exactly hand-writing — it was more like printing. But the words ran into each other. I decided to set aside the handwritten notes for some future date when I could spend time on them.'

Homer wrote something in his little book. 'But you think you can reconstruct the rest of the notes — the part Shipley dictated? All I want is the thought pattern — did Shipley write exclusively about people, for instance?'

'It was all about people, from the very

first words he dictated to me. I'll never forget the first sentence in the book. It went: *'This is a dirty book about dirty people!'*

Homer whistled. 'Mention any names?'

'Not very many in the dictated section. The second chapter — when the handwritten notes began — had many names.'

'Remember any of 'em?'

She paused. 'No, I didn't get into them much. I remember only Mike Gavano because he was in the first chapter.'

Homer said: 'I want you to do me a favor. I want you to go back home now and try to reconstruct those notes as carefully as you're able.'

'When do you want this?'

'As soon as possible, Eileen. Tonight, if you can manage.'

'I'll manage.' She smiled.

The old man helped her into her coat, and they started for the door. Homer suddenly called Nat back.

'I'd suggest, Tucker, that you stay at home with your daughter until she finishes that job.' He lowered his voice to a whisper. 'Tell no one about this and keep your eye on Eileen at all times.'

Nat was puzzled. 'What's up, Bull? What you drivin' at?'

'I don't want her left alone, you understand?'

Tucker's mouth fell open a bit. He closed it and said, 'Gotcha!'

I wished that I could have said the same.

6

Over the Hill to Nowhere

Homer got his idea, suddenly, in the hall.

'Hank,' he said, 'can you ski?'

'Me?' I snarled. 'I don't know a Christiana from a cheese blintze!'

'Oh, come,' Homer laughed 'It's not that bad now, is it?'

'It's worse, Homer. My mother was frightened by a pair of skis. I'm allergic to snow. I hate cold. And also, I can't ski well at all.'

'Would you rather walk?'

So now it was a choice.

'I'd rather walk in my sleep,' I groaned. 'I'm punchy from the lack of shut-eye. I'm also tired, hungry and even thirsty. What I need is a soft bed of feathers and a bottle of stuff.'

'Purely mental,' cooed Homer. 'Look — here's what you do.'

And I did it. I let myself out through

the kitchen door, well covered with all my sweaters and two of Homer's. Down in the garage there was a cluster of assorted skiing tools. I squirmed into a pair of brogans almost my size, and fitted them into a pair of the barrel staves.

I slid down the road cautiously, making good use of the two elongated icepicks. The road bent a bit some two hundred yards from the house, and it was there I spotted ski tracks, pointed into the woods at an oblique angle to the road. I dug into the icy ruts, skidded into a pratfall, dusted myself off and cursed Homer, Shipley and Nevin in a lump. Then I set my skis in the tracks ahead of me and eased into a slow drift along the snowy slope.

The prints were deep and clear and easy to follow. What did that mean? I caught myself thinking like a detective again, and it was ducky. Nevin must be a good skier, I figured, because the icepick marks alongside of the tracks appeared every third time I dug in with my poles. It meant that Nevin had moved himself in the slow, easy rhythm of a man who is experienced on the staves. The frequency of his pick pokes led me to deduce that he had been traveling at about twice the speed I made — and I wasn't doing at all badly.

Plunging thus into the dribs and drabs of my bad education in mathematics, I began to estimate our comparative speeds. For my own birdlike flight, I reckoned two or three miles an hour. That meant Nevin must have been going about six to ten miles an hour, or maybe more. Would it also mean that he might have been in a hurry? Why?

Nevin had taken quite a ride for himself. After the interminable hill there was another flat expanse of snow, another hill, steeper than the first, and then the end of the trail. I found myself on a broad cliff overlooking the valley. Far below, the road wound, a grey pencil smudge against the snow, now brilliant in the moonlight. I squatted on a tree stump and mopped my sweating brow. Wild goose chase.

I eased out of the staves and examined the small clearing. Nevin had done the same. I plucked three cigarette butts from the snow. He must have been waiting for someone. I lit the light and examined the footprints. He had stamped the clearing almost level. Was there a place where he stepped off into fresh snow? There was. I followed the prints for a few yards. They stopped, and so did I.

There was another set of footprints at this point. Another cigarette butt, too. I whistled through my teeth — this butt had lipstick marks!

For a while I deliberated my next move. Which trail to follow? We knew that Nevin had returned. Why not follow the new lead?

I slipped on my skis and pushed my way through the scrub pine, following the footsteps until they ended at fresh ski marks.

The mysterious skier couldn't have been expert. The trail led along the ridge to a wide clearing, then down a mild slope, where you skidded at an angle to the rolling hill, zigging and zagging at an easy pace to a broad plateau, where even an amateur could ski with confidence.

The trail crossed the plateau and ran a

good distance to the north, as though the skier might have been searching for an easier way down. Finally, in a narrow cut between giant trees, the trail dipped downward, coasted toward the road and ended.

I crossed the road and peered along the edge, but whoever made those tracks must have finished his trip on foot. There were no ski marks in the glistening snow on either side of the road. Perhaps the mysterious skier had walked back to the house, carrying his skis. My deductions made me laugh out loud. The skier might have finished the distance to the house still skiing on the road, and thus have left no marks. The strain of simple deduction was tying my feeble noggin in knots. I shook my head free of thought and slid off the road onto the field, to take the short cut to the garage. I pushed nimbly into the snow in a final burst of speed that left my arms limp.

My legs came alive, slowly, while I examined the rack of ski equipment. All the skis were dry. The icepicks, too, showed no signs of recent contact with

Jack Frost. I puttered around the garage, looking for shoes. There was another pair, obviously a man's — but they were as dry as my throat. It came to me, suddenly, that ski boots weren't usually left in garages. Nevin had worn his into the house. Whoever had met him on the hill walked into the house with her boots on. Who? Grace Lawrence? Olympe? Eileen?

I entered the kitchen through that garage.

The Mintons were bending over the kitchen table, deep in a pot of coffee and a table full of sandwiches. Lester scowled at me over his left shoulder, but continued to eat. I saw Minnie Minton's leg crack his shins, and he jerked to his feet, blubbering.

'Something to eat, sir?' he glugged through a mouthful of Hank and cheese and who knows what.

'Get the man a chair!' Minnie squealed. 'Won't you ever learn nothing?'

He pulled over a chair for me and I sat down heavily, with half a sandwich in my craw before my frozen seat hit the chair.

I gave Minnie my best schoolboy grin. 'Minnie, you're the best cook east of the

Mississippi. Where'd you learn to make turkey like this?'

It hit home. Minnie fiddled with her spoon and wriggled coyly. 'Now that's nice. That's nice,' she chirped. 'Ain't heard talk like that since I worked for Mrs. Archer. You heard of her?'

I shook my head.

Lester shifted uneasily on his feet.

'Sit down, Lester,' I told him. 'I'm just folks.'

He gawked at Minnie.

'You heard him,' she shrilled. 'How many times I have to tell you we ain't servants in the kitchen? People visit in the kitchen, they got to act natural with servants. No cause to fuss in the kitchen, Mrs. Archer always said. She came in and had tea with me many's the time, just as natural as you please.' Minnie leaned toward me confidentially. 'Lester ain't never going to learn, Mr. — ?'

'MacAndrew.'

'MacAndrew? Irish, is it?' Minnie clucked delightedly. 'I'm part Irish. One half, I am.' She paused to remember what she had been saying. 'I was saying Lester ain't never going to learn. It's been four years I'm learning him things. Four years I'm learning him butlering, but it's like the saying goes about learning an old dog new tricks. I'm giving up. The man was never cut to butler. Chauffeuring, now, that's Lester's line.' She threw him a look of scorn. 'You hear me, Lester? Sit down!'

Lester squatted gingerly.

'Where'd you chauffeur in Brooklyn, Lester?'

'Columbia Heights,' he muttered.

'Swank. Who was the lucky boss?'

There was a pause while Lester slurped coffee. 'Fellow with a funny name,' said Minnie. 'Wasn't it Window, Lester? Minnow? Belinda?'

I caught a quick flash of fury in Lester's pig eyes. But Minnie didn't.

'Ginder, was it?' She was losing her patience.

'Can't remember,' he said.

Minnie plucked the name off the ceiling.

'Pindo!' she shrilled. 'It was Pindo, wasn't it?'

Pindo! Could it be the Pindo I thought

it was? No wonder Lester didn't want to remember. There was only one important Pindo in Brooklyn.

'Had dozens of cars,' Minnie went on. 'Lester courted me in style, he did. Every time we went out, it was a ride for Minnie in a different car. Once in an Eyetalian one even — oh, what a grand thing it was, that Eyetalian car.'

'Isotta?' I asked Lester. 'Your boss must have been in the chips.'

'He was pretty rich.'

'Made his dough in the slot-machine racket, didn't he?'

'I don't know nuthin' about where he made his dough,' Lester snapped. 'I drove for the family. Mostly his wife and daughter.'

'Tina?'

'He only had one daughter.'

'That's right,' I said. 'Underworld society, eh, Lester?'

Lester didn't answer. Minnie flitted to the stove with the empty percolator.

'You'll be wanting another cup, fresh,' she said. 'Git up, Lester! Mr. MacAndrew might be wanting a drink of brandy, too, him just being out in the cold. You know where the brandy is, you big fool! Get your legs movin' after it!'

Lester got up slowly. He didn't want to move.

'Make it Scotch,' I told him.

He grunted and left.

'Not that I need the Scotch.' I winked. 'After your elegant coffee. Your coffee will do me fine any time, Minnie.'

'Will it now, sir?' Minnie's grin wrinkled her lean jaw. 'That's what I always say. I always say there ain't nothin' better than a good coffee, after the cold. Not that Scotch is wrong, sir. Not that Scotch is wrong at all. But you can't beat coffee, now can you?' She sighed over the sink. 'Mr. Shipley, he was a great one for my coffee, too.'

'He built a fine ski trail out there,' I said. 'Did his guests use it much?'

'Indeed they did,' she said. 'All of 'em favored the sport, though I can't see why. Mostly it's fallin', from the look of it.'

'With me it is,' I laughed. 'But Nevin, now, he's a fancy skier. I saw him come down the hill a while ago. He's an expert.

Came down with a woman — just like two birds, they were. I wonder who the woman was?'

'Ah, that must have been Eileen,' she said. 'Ain't she pretty?'

I hid my amazement in another sandwich. 'Nope. Didn't look like Eileen to me. Don't the other ladies ski?'

'Indeed they do,' Minnie sniffed. 'But not like Eileen, though they're fair, both of 'em.'

'Looked more like Miss Lawrence to me,' I said. 'Was she out there this afternoon?'

'I couldn't say, me not bein' in here most of the time.'

Lester came in with the drinks.

'Did you notice?' she snapped. 'You see, I was up in my room nappin', till half an hour ago. Lester would know. Wouldn't you know, Lester? Speak up!'

'Didn't see nobody but Mr. Nevin.'

'You were in the kitchen when he came in?' I asked.

'In the garage, cleanin' skis. I cleaned his stuff off.'

'Find any of the other skis wet?'

'They was all wet.'

'Phuh!' scoffed Minnie. 'How would you know? You're full of brandy, I suppose, from the cellar.'

Lester growled. 'That don't matter. Them skis was wet, I tell ya.'

'Keep your shirt on,' I said, and gulped the dregs of my coffee. I thanked Minnie for her hospitality and walked into the hall. My watch told me four-fifteen. I had been gone only an hour. There was the buzz of talk from the living room. I crept softly through the dining room and up the stairs.

Grace's room was easy to spot. She had brought plenty of luggage, brightly banded in the latest manner and festooned with gilt monograms, too large to miss.

I blew my nose, lit a cigarette, and dropped to my knees for a quick survey under the bed. No boots. Then the door clicked open.

'Lose your collar button, jerk?'

I took a wild chance.

It was Grace.

'Look,' I said, making meek with my eyes, 'I only wanted to find out if you

80

were skiing this afternoon. I was looking for your ski boots.'

She raised a penciled eyebrow. 'Don't hand me that!'

'On the level,' I said.

'Why couldn't you ask me? Why couldn't Homer ask me?'

'Homer doesn't know a thing about this,' I pleaded.

She allowed me a thin quizzical smile. 'I don't know why I should believe you, MacAndrew, but I do.'

'And the answer?'

'The answer is no,' she said. 'Any more questions?'

I wanted to ask her for a gander at her ski boots. Why should she tell me the truth?

Grace read my mind. 'You don't believe me?'

'Sure I do.'

'You're a bad liar, MacAndrew.' She bounced into the bathroom and came back with her ski boots. They were dry.

'I'm sorry,' I said.

'Skip it,' she laughed. 'And give Homer my love.'

I backed into the hall and bumped my fanny on somebody's bay window. It was Trum, steaming.

'What's this?' he growled, glaring at me.

I felt like the sharp end of a bedroom triangle.

'Will those sketches be enough?' Grace cooed.

'Plenty,' I managed.

'What sketches?' grumbled Trum.

'Mr. MacAndrews is an artist, sugar. He came up to make a few preliminary sketches for a portrait.'

'Yeah.' I patted my pocket. 'These'll be plenty, till I get back to town.'

Grace grabbed Trum's arm and pinched his fleshy jowls. 'Is Duggy jealous? After all, Mr. MacAndrew only does heads.'

Trum took the oil and harrumphed. 'Fine idea. Have to let you do my head, too, sometime.'

'It would be a pleasure.' I bowed, and left them to each other.

In the hall, Olympe Deming turned the corner, on the way to her room. My research was over.

7

Nicky Speaks Out

Homer was in the living room with Nicky English, Stanley Nevin, Cunningham and Gavano. Swink remained in the doorway, squinting into the room over his pipe.

Cunningham was saying: 'I've been up here many, many times, Bull. Shipley and I were old friends.'

'But this was a business trip?'

'Indirectly, yes,' said Cunningham. 'I brought Mr. Trum up on business. As you know, Trum controls International Tobacco, and has a great deal to say about how most of his brands are advertised. I had sold Trum the idea of having Shipley do a series of drawings for some advertisements.'

'Then Shipley knew Trum was coming?'

'Oh, yes. Hugo has entertained Trum before.'

'How about Miss Lawrence?'

Cunningham ran his fingers through

his mop of varnished hair. 'What do you mean?'

'Was she invited, too?'

'Yes. She — ah — came up as Trum's guest.'

'Interesting,' murmured Homer. 'And the business deal — how did it go?'

Cunningham smiled. 'It didn't. Shipley absolutely refused to do the type of drawing Trum wanted. You see, we wanted female stuff — something that might outdo the Pretty Woman. Hugo didn't care for the idea — not under his signature, at least.'

'Why was that?'

'He claimed that it would cheapen his reputation. He was quite firm about it.'

'You can go now, if you like, Mr. Cunningham.'

'I'd rather stay.'

Homer turned to Gavano. 'You're next, Mike. How'd you happen to be up here this weekend?'

Gavano showed his gold teeth. 'Hugo and me, we was old chums.'

'He sent you an invitation?'

'I don't need no invitations. I told you

Hugo and me was chums, see?'

Homer smiled. 'We're not getting anywhere, Gavano. How long have you known Shipley?'

'I can't remember. A long time. Ever since he's been makin' moola. Hugo put me on for a bodyguard, after he got up in the big time. I been with him maybe five years, off and on.'

'He's lying,' Nicky snapped. 'I didn't see him up here the last time I was here.'

'Keep your drawers on, punk,' sneered Gavano. 'Did I say I stayed here all the time?' He lowered his eyes in the manner of a Steig pug. 'I come up when Hugo calls me, see? This week he calls me up, so I come.'

'Did Shipley tell you why he wanted you? Was he afraid of anybody?'

'Hugo never says much. I just sit around and keep my eyes open.'

Nicky laughed lightly.

'How much did Shipley pay you?' Homer asked.

'He doesn't pay me any regular wages. We're old chums, see? What Hugo gives me, I take.'

'Did you ever meet any of these guests before, Mike?'

Gavano's rat eyes roved the room. 'I never mingles with Hugo's guests when I come up.' He pointed to Nicky. 'But you ask me if I ever meet any of these guys before, hah? Yeah — I meet this punk English. Once, but not up here, see?'

'He's talking about Brooklyn now.' Nicky leered. 'He's trying to tell you he met me once three years ago, when I blew the lid off his stinking protection racket. Isn't that right, Gavano?'

Gavano's eyes were pinpoints of hate. 'That's right, you half-pint heel! Mike Gavano ain't forgot about that yet, see?'

'Better button your mouth, Mike,' Nicky said coolly. 'Some Boy Scouts in Brooklyn are sending me letters about other activities.'

'Someday you're gonna wake up in a barrel of cement, Nicky!' Gavano's big fists were white in his lap. 'You through with me, Bull?'

Homer let him go, and Nevin left a minute later.

Nicky said: 'Don't ask me, Bull — I'll

tell you. I was up here once before, in 1936 — in the fall. I never again visited Hugo Shipley. Why? Because I hated his guts! But you probably read all about it.'

'Let's see,' mused Homer. 'Wasn't that the time of the Hugo Shipley cowboy act? I seem to recall something about a well-known illustrator chasing a well-known columnist down a well-known street in New York — with a gun.'

'Two guns,' corrected Cunningham. 'That incident took place just one week *after* Nicky's visit, didn't it, Nicky?'

Nicky's face went white. 'You ought to know!'

Cunningham smiled archly. 'How can I forget?'

I couldn't forget, either, now that I remembered. Every newspaper in New York, even the *Times*, had run that story. But it was the tabloids that played it for all it was worth. Abner Gillray, the rusty-headed cameraman from the *Globe*, happened to be staggering out of a bar when the chase began. Abner caught every phase of it, in fine, sharp blacks and whites, including the curling smoke from one of Shipley's guns. ARTIST CHASES ENGLISH DOWN FIFTH AVENUE, screamed the headlines. PEEPING TOM CHASED BY FAMOUS ILLUSTRATOR! TWO-GUN SHIPLEY ALMOST GETS HIS MAN!

The details remained indelible in my memory, thanks to the nimble pen of Shelley Stark, fiction man, who sold the incident (with a story built around it) to the waiting cameras in Hollywood.

At that famous party, Nicky English, squatting at Shipley's studio door, spotted the red silk of someone else's wife in Hugo's arms. And printed it!

Hugo, full of righteous wrath at this insult to one of his cash customers, brooded over a gallon of liquor until he felt ripe enough for two guns. He chased Nicky from Park Avenue in the Fifties to a taxicab on the corner of Broadway and Forty-Eighth Street — a half-mile sprint, no matter how you figure it.

The newspapers played the story for laughs, but smart talk had it that Shipley would have really plugged English that night, if he had caught him. He was tanked to the ears and ready for a showdown with

Nicky. Shipley didn't enjoy the notoriety, even though the name of the lady was never really printed. The pithy paragraph had only said something like: '*What ad exec's pretty wife snuggled with what illustrator on a weekend party in W — ?*'

What advertising executives were up in Woodstock on that memorable weekend? Hoagy Bellows was one. But Hoagy's wife was an underslung bag, married in the lean days. Shipley wouldn't ever make passes at Helen Bellows.

Cunningham was there, too. Was Cunningham sure of his wife? Cunningham was an ex-footballer from Yale, six foot something or other and needing no gun to squash Nicky English. Cunningham sat tight and let the scandal blow itself out. He wasn't mad at all. Was it because he knew his wife? Mimi Cunningham, nee Mimi Lavere (third from the left in the *Gaieties* chorus) was short and sweet and rounded in the best places. It must have been Mimi. It probably was, because Bruce Cunningham divorced her a year later. Was Mimi the answer? Nobody knew.

Of course, there were other suspects — wild stories told in the gin mills about the dame he really was bundling that night. The mystery died deep in the ads and I never knew the last word. I'm strictly a headline reader, except for *True Stories of Crime, Terry and the Pirates,* and an item called *Crosstown.*'

'Gentlemen,' soothed Homer, 'you're moving too fast for poor little me. What I don't understand is why Hugo Shipley waited for four years before inviting his favorite columnist again.'

'Who said he was invited?' Cunningham cracked.

Nicky laughed out loud. 'You advertising apes think everybody lies as much as you do. Suppose I tell you I have an invitation?'

'I wouldn't believe you!'

Nicky let it pass and turned to Homer. 'Is there any law that says I must answer questions while this crumb heckles me?'

Homer said: 'I'm afraid I'll have to ask you to leave, Cunningham.'

Cunningham rose. 'It'll be a pleasure.'

Nicky waited until he left the room.

'I wasn't fooling, Bull,' he said. 'I came here by invitation, of course. I have the invitation upstairs, whenever you care to see it.'

'It can wait,' said Homer. 'I believe you. Tell me, Nicky, did you ever bother to ask Shipley why you were invited? You and he don't make for a congenial weekend.'

'I bothered,' snapped English. 'You're damn well right, I bothered. The minute I met him in the studio I asked him. It was a story,' he said.'

'What sort of a story?'

'Shipley wouldn't say any more, except that I should take a look around — and enjoy myself. I suppose he meant that I should watch his guests for a story. I'm not sure.'

'That was all?'

Nicky thought a bit. 'No, that wasn't all. He told me he would have something hot for me by Tuesday night!'

There was a silence. Tonight was Monday. Death had closed Hugo's mouth.

Homer relit his cigar. 'I wonder whether he might have meant that you would find a story among his guests.'

Nicky shook his head almost violently. 'That's nonsense! I've printed loads of stuff on most of these people. I mean Cunningham, Trum, Gavano, and even Grace Lawrence. The possibility of more dirt about them wouldn't intrigue me — and Shipley knew it.'

'Oh, come now,' said Homer, beaming, 'your column isn't run that way, Nicky. Why try to kid me? Anything fresh about these people would be printable, wouldn't it?'

'I didn't say that it wouldn't be printable! I said that I don't think Shipley would have called me up here for that type of story!'

'Are you trying to say that his story was beyond gossip — that it was real news?'

'Exactly!'

'Do you mean that Shipley knew that he'd commit suicide?'

'Perhaps.'

'And the *suicide* was to be your story?'

'That's screwy!' Nick said. 'But if he *didn't* commit suicide, it might have been because somebody didn't want him to spill his little yarn for publication!'

'Nobody ever suggested before this that Shipley didn't commit suicide, Nicky. What makes you think he didn't?'

Nicky brayed. 'Don't make me laugh, Bull! What have you been doing all afternoon — playing Professor Quiz?'

Homer eyed him soberly. 'I've been conducting an examination before the inquest.'

'Then you think Shipley was a suicide?'

'I haven't reached any conclusion, Nicky. Have you?'

Nicky leaned forward.

'Can't I play detective, too, Bull? Do I look like a sucker? Maybe I've got an angle on this business that's escaped the syndicate Sherlock, eh?'

Homer shrugged. 'Maybe you have.'

'If I have, I'm playing it alone — my way. This thing is going to break in my column, if little Nicky has the right angle.'

'And if Nicky's wrong?'

Nicky opened his mouth in a smirk, but he closed it fast. Gavano walked into the room, and behind him Stanley Nevin and Trum.

93

'See you in the funny papers,' whispered Nicky on the way out.

'Not if I see you first,' mumbled Homer to the end of his cigar.

We strolled into the library together, where I told Homer my story, including the cigarette butt (which he pocketed), the snack with the Mintons and the search up in Grace's room. Homer blew hot and cold.

'The business on the hill doesn't seem worth much,' he said. 'After all, anybody might have been up on the hill this afternoon. Nevin may have had a date with — ah — any one of the women — Eileen, or Olympe, or Grace.'

'That's why I followed the lead,' I explained. 'I thought it might be important. Anyhow, it wasn't Grace.'

'Of course not. Nevin's not her type. He grinned. 'Grace runs to the fat boy, sugar daddy type.'

When I mentioned Pindo and Lester, he blew hot, and jerked out his notebook.

'There you have something — something that I wasn't able to squeeze out of Lester. Pindo's a notorious Brooklyn racketeer. So is Gavano. There may be a fit somewhere.'

'And don't forget Pindo's daughter, Tina.'

'Not for a minute will I forget Tina, sonny. I'll get a line on these people when I call the Shtunk — I'm sure he can ferret them all.'

'Even Tina?'

'The Shtunk gets around. I have an idea — ' He nibbled on his eraser and stared at the rug. 'But I wonder? I wonder what Nicky knows?'

I wondered, too. 'Think we can get to him?'

Homer shook his head. 'Nicky's still a reporter at heart, Hank. He'll save his little angle, his piece of information, until he's sure it's useless. But I'll have to stop guessing now.' He patted his vest. 'I find it hard to think on an empty stomach.'

8

Comic Strip Tease

I was eating again, this time in the library. We had drooled through a table full of roast Hank with the savor of cloves and the tang of wine and now sat back nibbling a cheese that smelled bad enough to enjoy.

He tossed me a few pages. 'When you begin to read,' Homer added, 'you'll be reading the answer to our first and most important question: 'Who last saw Shipley alive?''

I began to read.

7:15–7:20 MINNIE MINTON
Minnie says she last saw Shipley standing near his easel when she passed through the hall at this time. She had a quick squint into the studio, but because of the angle (and the fact that she was only passing through the hall on the way to her room), Minnie could

not say whether Shipley was alone. When she returned from her room, sometime later, the door was closed.

7:16-7:20 STANLEY NEVIN

Nevin dropped in for a chat with Shipley at this time. They had cocktail and discussed art for a while. Nevin says that Shipley seemed in good spirits, and made a date to meet him in New York during the week. (Something about an Illustrators' Show at Radio City. Check this.) Nevin excused himself after a while — had a bad headache. Went to his room after about ten minutes with Shipley.

7:40 NICKY ENGLISH

Enter Nicky English, who reports that he went to the studio to try to pump Shipley about that story. Says Shipley didn't act at all strange — but hinted 'that he may have been a bit nervous. It's hard to tell with Shipley.' Had a cocktail and asked Shipley about the story. Shipley seemed almost ready to say something when —

7:50 (APP'X) LESTER MINTON
(by Lester and Nicky)
Lester knocked at the door to tell Shipley that Eileen Tucker was waiting to take dictation. Shipley walked to the door and told Lester to have Eileen wait in the library until 8:30. Lester went away to tell Eileen. Nicky remained. Tried for the story again. Shipley said: 'Come back a little after nine.' Nicky left just as —

7:55 GRACE LAWRENCE
walked in. Grace, too, had a cocktail. (Shipley must have had a barrel of it in the room.) Grace says she doesn't remember how long she stayed. She admired his sketch on the easel. Shipley seemed nervous, unpoised, not his usual self. Rubbed his forehead and complained of a 'filthy headache.' Usually a brilliant conversationalist — but this time the talk dragged. She asked him whether he felt well. Said he did, but didn't look it. She, too, asked him whether he would be represented in Illustrators' Show in New York. Shipley

said 'yes,' but didn't seem interested. Then, in walked —

8:15 MIKE GAVANO

(Grace left in a hurry — she can't stand Gavano.) Mike says he had a short one. Came in to find out what Shipley wanted him to do for the rest of the weekend. (Doesn't explain why he did nothing up until then.) Shipley just told him to keep his eyes open. Mike reports that he looked sick, down in the mouth, on edge, jumpy. Shipley ordered Mike out when —

8:30 LESTER MINTON AND EILEEN TUCKER

Punctual Lester appeared at the studio door with Eileen. He and Gavano walked out together. Eileen says Shipley waved her to a seat and began to pace the room, trying to start his dictation. It came slowly. He smoked three or four cigarettes, nervously. Told her to cross out what he had dictated and started all over again. Rubbed his forehead (?). Finally sat down and ran his hands through his hair. Seemed either sick, or a little bit drunk. At least sick. Got up and tried to dictate again, when they were interrupted by —

8:45 (?) CUNNINGHAM AND TRUM
(Shipley told Eileen to report the next morning, and she left.) Both Cunningham and Trum report same story: Cunningham (whose agency handles Trum's cigarette account) pleaded with Shipley to do the type of drawings they wanted. Shipley agreed to do the ads if Trum wouldn't insist on half-nude women. Shipley suggested studies of typical American Woman heads. Trum said that was old-fashioned, insisted on sexy dames to compete with Petty ads. Argued back and forth, but not too violently. Shipley's heart didn't seem in the fight. Seemed tired to both these gentlemen. Asked time to think it over. Trum promised more dough, if Shipley would do the job, and left, leaving Cunningham to try to sell Shipley the idea.

(9: PLUS TRUM LEAVES) CUNNINGHAM CONTINUES:

Cunningham continued to talk, but Shipley seemed distracted. Cunningham gave up at about 9:15, when —

9:15 (?) NICKY ENGLISH

knocked. (Nicky had returned at about 9, but heard Trum and Cunningham arguing with Shipley — went to library for a few moments. Returned at about 9:15.) Says Cunningham seemed angry as hell when he walked out of studio. Glared at Shipley on way out. Nicky once again tried to get that story. Once again interrupted, this time by —

9:40 OLYMPE DEMING *by* (NICKY ENGLISH)

Who came in and seemed ready to wait all night for Nicky to leave. Nicky stayed on until almost 10:30. They all talked small talk, Shipley trying hard to be sociable. Nicky gave up all hope of seeing Shipley alone, left the two together at about 10:30. Went upstairs to his room. (*Might he have remained at keyhole, true to his trade?* Check possibilities.)

Olympe remained with Shipley to talk about the Illustrators' Show. Wanted to find out which drawings Shipley wanted exhibited. Shipley didn't seem at all interested in the show. She insisted canvases had to be ready by Tuesday in Radio City. Shipley said it could wait until tomorrow. Seemed anxious for her to leave, somehow. Complained of a headache. She asked him why he didn't go to sleep. Answered that he had some work to do. Olympe left just before eleven.

I threw down the notes.

'Cozy as hell, Homer. That studio must have seemed like the Grand Central Station to Shipley last night. He was visited by every one of his guests.'

'And yet,' said Homer, 'with all those visits, there's a gap to fill. Olympe is positive that she looked at her watch at eleven o'clock, when she left Shipley alone in the studio. He died at eleven-thirty.'

'You think one of 'em came back

during that half hour?'

'Why only one? I can see many reasons for several of our characters returning to Shipley. Nicky English, for instance. Nicky may have wanted to plead for that story again. Cunningham might have returned to talk about the artwork. Gavano for some reason of his own.' He sighed. 'It's all very confusing.'

'You're telling me.' I couldn't see where the road led. 'Homer, you're a genius if you can twist this one into a murder.'

Homer didn't acknowledge my tease. He tilted the bottle of *Suduiraut* into a glass, sipped it and played with the second stack of notes. 'Here's some more hash to confuse us, Hank. I've boiled down most of my shorthand notes from the conference in the living room. Like to hear them?'

I nodded. I can't read shorthand.

'We must begin with Eileen Tucker, and read from left to right around the room. I have a feeling that Eileen was dragged into this mess only because she happened to be taking notes on Shipley's whacky book. There's nothing of any importance in her testimony, except the book business, which we'll explore later. We'll have to wait for her summary of the first chapter of the book before we include her in.'

'In *what*?' I objected. 'This isn't a murder case.'

'Not yet,' said Homer. 'Not yet.'

The fog lifted as I gulped my wine. I couldn't see Eileen a suspect in a suicide. Yet there was nothing illegal about the idea. Why had Homer left her hanging until the first chapter of Shipley's book was redone from memory? It came to me suddenly that Homer might already suppose Shipley had been murdered. How? I couldn't begin to imagine.

'How about Nat Tucker?' I asked.

'Nat is an interesting character . . . the sort of character a good writer can't overlook. He was at home when Lester came for him. He dressed quickly while Lester waited, and then came up to the house.'

I interrupted. 'But before that, he flew through the air, dissolved through the studio walls in a grey mist, shot Shipley and then faded back outside?'

Homer puckered a grin and rubbed his jowls. 'Let's not gag it up, Hank. If there's been a murder, it'll be as simple as a cartoonist's noggin.'

I bowed. 'I can't wait.'

Homer went on. 'Next is Nevin. Nevin makes a fine figure of a hero for a *Ladies' Home Journal* serial. He smells sweet and pure and tainted with the attar of Lifebuoy. We've got nothing on Nevin. Nevin says he came down as soon as he heard the shot. Or rather, he *imagines* he came down immediately. He was asleep, dressed; upstairs when the shot awakened him. We can allow a period of mental confusion, because a man awakened by a gunshot need not necessarily know what woke him, or would he? Probably not — by Nevin's own admission. He reports he heard footsteps running down the hall. He jumped to the door, saw Grace running down the steps in her nightie — '

'Lucky boy,' I said.

' — and followed her into the studio.'

'What about the skiing?'

'Nothing. Nevin admitted he was skiing. Lester cleaned his skis, and Nevin walked into the library, where we met him. We can forget the skiing for a while. It doesn't fit into any pattern.'

'What does?' I moaned.

'You can't have a pattern without pieces. Let me finish throwing pieces at your intelligence. Next piece is Grace.'

I gave him the grin he was waiting for. At least he was being realistic, adding Grace to the patter. But I shouldn't have been surprised. Time and again, Homer had proven himself feisty about crime. His fat frame was deceptive. There was nothing soft about Homer. Oh, sure, he was a softy — a kind, tender and lovable little guy, away from the smell of blood and the trail of mayhem. He was a good brother to his seven sisters. He sent flowers and telegrams on Mamma's Day. He loved babies, kissed little girls, gave them pennies, and I have even caught him sobbing at a Shirley Temple tear jerker.

'I suppose,' I said 'that Grace was in the arms of — ah — Morpheus, when the shot was fired?'

'Not exactly. No two alibis in this party.'

'But didn't Nevin report her running down the hall in her nightie? She must have come from her bedroom.'

'You mean a bedroom, but that isn't important now. Grace says she was in her own bedroom, and we'll believe her for a while. She's gone literary, Hank. The little lady was deep in the arms of Hemingway, helping him toll the bell, when the big noise came.'

'Then, of course, she sprang into instant action?'

'As instant as it can ever be for Grace. She leaped into her sheerest silk robe, probably grabbed for the mascara on the way to the door, and shook her plump self down to the studio door.'

'She didn't even stop to show Nevin her bedroom eyes?'

'She saw nothing all the way down. Terrified, she says. All agog about the shot. But she did say that she heard a door slam from upstairs.'

'Nevin's?'

'How could she know? I don't see Nevin as the door-slamming type. We have our door slammer — we have two of 'em. Cunningham slammed, and so did Nicky English.' Homer paused for a long puff. 'Anyhow, Lester crashed the door in when she reached the last step. When she arrived in the studio, she saw Olympe and Minnie Minton out cold and Lester gawking down at the corpse.'

We were interrupted by Swink, who walked into the library with his last bite of food still rolling in his long jaw.

'I got that information you wanted, Bull.'

Homer gathered his notes and stuffed them into the fat folds of his jacket.

'You asked them all?'

'Yep. There was no light in the studio when the body was found. I have it from Lester, Minnie, Miss Deming, Miss Lawrence and Stanley Nevin. Nevin switched on the light after he arrived.'

Homer was writing again.

'That means Nicky English, Trum, Cunningham and Gavano walked into a lighted room?'

'That's the story.'

Homer leaned on his elbow, doodling the napkin. He came awake suddenly.

'Get Miss Deming for me, Swink.'

'Now?' asked Swink, eyeing the wine.

Homer showed him the door. 'The plot thickens,' he said to the door, closing it gently.

I dropped into a chair and massaged my scalp. 'Oh, to be in Flatbush on a night like this.'

9

Olympe's Game

'Olympe teases my imagination,' said Homer.

'Is that all?'

Swink led Olympe into the room, and we jerked ourselves out of dreamland. Homer put her at her ease with a glass of Suduiraut. She gave him an icy smile.

'I've waited to see you alone,' Homer began. 'There are a few questions I thought you might like to answer informally.'

'How considerate of you,' she said evenly.

Homer showed her his teeth in a smile. 'Have you worked for Mr. Shipley long, Miss Deming?'

She didn't wait to think. 'I've been up here for two weeks. Two weeks tonight.'

'Did you know Mr. Shipley before you came?'

'Casually.'

'How did he happen to hire you?'

'I was a model,' she answered quickly. 'I worked in the Powers Agency, doing fashions. John Powers introduced me to Shipley and I took the job he offered.'

I could almost read Homer's mind as he scribbled. He was making a note about this last statement. If Olympe was really a model, Grace might have known her before the weekend party.

'Then the pay must have been better than you earned freelancing as a model?'

'No, it wasn't.' She paused, nettled. 'But the future was brighter. There's no future in modelling.'

I knew Homer would mark this down as an obvious lie. There was plenty of future in modelling for a woman like Olympe. Was there a greater future for her than the possibility of Hollywood, or the stage, or an easy marriage into wealth?

'What did you do for Shipley?' Homer asked the question without a smile. There was no hint of innuendo.

'I was beginning to learn how to take care of his business matters. I expected to be his agent eventually.'

111

'Do you type?'

'I do not.' She raised her eyes and levelled them at him. 'Nor do I do shorthand. Mr. Shipley knew these things. He thought them unnecessary.'

Homer toyed with his pencil for a moment. 'You didn't pose for Shipley?'

'Certainly not!'

'Then what were your duties?'

'I'd only begun to learn them. I managed the household details and attended to all matters of business — correspondence, and so on.'

Homer didn't seem anxious to make an issue of her private life with Shipley. 'Tell me what happened last night, Miss Deming, from the time you last saw Shipley alive.'

Her eyes brightened with the horror of memory. She twisted her handkerchief in her hands and stared at it.

'I left Mr. Shipley at almost exactly eleven o'clock and walked into the library. I wanted a book to take upstairs with me, because I wasn't very sleepy. I sat in the library, thumbing through several books of pictures. I must have been there for a half an hour. Then I heard the shot.'

'You met nobody from the time you left the studio until you heard the gun go off?'

'Nobody.'

'Go on, Miss Deming.'

'I ran into the hall and through the dining room. The studio door was locked.'

Homer interrupted again. 'Why did you run to the studio? The shot might have come from any part of the house, mightn't it?'

Olympe reddened. 'I don't know why. Intuition, I guess.'

'Are you sure there isn't another reason?'

She bit her lip. 'There was a reason. I was worried, afraid that Hu — Mr. Shipley might have met somebody and got hurt.'

'Met who?'

'Oh, I don't know!' Her voice rose. 'He never told me that he expected anybody. But he acted so — so queerly, I just ran to the studio instinctively, I guess.'

'Was Mr. Shipley afraid of any of his guests?'

'If he was, he never told me of his fears.'

There was a pause, and Olympe rose.

'One more question, Miss Deming. Are you quite sure that the light was out in the studio when you entered with the Mintons?'

'Quite sure.'

Homer found still another question in his little black book. He reached into his jacket and handed Olympe his invitation.

'Did you type that, Miss Deming?'

'No. Mr. Shipley sent all the invitations himself.'

'Good!' said Homer. 'And thank you very much, Miss Deming.' He bowed her out of the room.

Swink said: 'Funny, her runnin' right to the studio, now ain't it?'

'She's holding something back,' I suggested.

Homer prodded me in the ribs. 'Keen thinking, MacAndrews. I agree with you.'

'I don't get it,' said Swink. 'Don't get it at all.'

'You will. Where did you find her, Swink?'

'In the studio.'

'Alone?'

Swink nodded.

Homer started for the door, grabbing my elbow. We avoided the main hall, and left the house through the terrace door. There was a small light burning in the studio!

Homer doubled his speed, and we circled the house to enter again by way of the kitchen. We slowed to a walk in the studio hall, and stopped in the doorway.

Olympe Deming was bent over Shipley's big desk, her hands deep in a drawer!

'Did you find it, Miss Deming?' asked Homer.

She straightened, and her hands dropped to her sides awkwardly. 'Oh!' she whispered. 'You startled me.' She pointed to the disarray on the desktop. 'I was just looking for some bills — some old bills Mr. Shipley wanted me to pay before he — '

Homer leaned on the desk. 'Why not tell me the truth, Miss Deming?'

'But I am!' Her voice shook.

Homer shrugged. 'Very well, if you say so.'

Olympe brushed the papers into a drawer and left us. Homer blew air through his teeth and bounced to the door. He leaned it into place and jerked a chair up to keep it closed.

'Olympe had the right idea, Hank,' said he, nudging me over to the desk. 'Here, help me with this top drawer.'

Shipley's desk was as big as a ping pong table. We tugged the massive top drawer out of its socket and lifted it to the desktop. It was a shambles. Loose bills, advertisements, and the hodgepodge of miscellaneous art supplies filled it to overflowing.

Homer started with the big checkbook, motioning me to wade into the stuff. 'Salvage anything that looks interesting.'

He dug into the checkbook, thumbing the pages slowly and easily, in the manner of an income tax collector. Three times he paused to insert slips of paper, whistling as he jammed them in. After the fourth time, he paused.

'Hugo made withdrawals of twenty-five hundred bucks each month for the past four months,' he said. 'And marked each withdrawal 'personal.''

'That's a lot of potatoes for spending money, isn't it?'

He made an entry in his notebook. 'The last withdrawal of that amount was made on last Friday.'

'Great jumping ginch!' I blatted. 'Did Swink find any cash on him after the suicide?'

'Not twenty-five hundred bucks.'

He grabbed a sheaf of assorted bills and gave them the thumb, pausing to pluck one from the batch occasionally. When he had finished, Homer tucked the few bills he had salvaged into his pocket and turned to me.

'Find anything interesting?'

'Only ads.'

We finished the big drawer and went on to the others. It was the usual mess found in every artist's studio — a ton of old stationery, envelopes, scrap paper, discarded drawing board, aged sketching research and a few old finished pieces of artwork.

Homer closed the last drawer and rested his fat fanny against the desktop. 'Whatever it was that Olympe wanted,' he sighed, 'isn't in this desk.' He let his eyes flit over the room. 'You're an artist, Hank.

If you wanted to hide something — a slip of paper, perhaps — where would you cache it?'

'That's a tough one, Professor Quiz. My little mouse nest isn't this ornate. Aside from that, I've never had anything to hide.'

I looked around. There was a small drawing table, probably used by Shipley for preliminary layouts. It gave me an idea. I crossed the room and gave it the once-over.

'Here.' I pointed. 'Shipley was human, after all. He's thumbtacked a raft of junk on his drawing table. What are we looking for?'

Homer bounced over and surveyed the table. There were dozens of small sketches pinned along the top. Under these, odd-sized strips of paper, smeared with watercolor and lampblack wash. Homer unpinned the scraps and began to examine their backsides. He paused to stare at a small square sheet.

'Bingo! We're halfway home, sonny. Read this!'

He handed me a sheet of notepaper, of

the type that women use for invitations to teas, and the brief messages of feminine correspondence. Neatly typed, the message read:

> him now, dear. It will save
> heartache later.
> With all my love,
> Winnie-the-pooh.

'Halfway?' I said. 'This looks like the last sentence of a letter.'

Homer stared at the board. 'Quite true. But if we could find the other half — the other sheet — we'd be finished with our search.'

'Then we'd better give up, Homer. If he used his half of the letter for testing paints, the other half has long since hit bottom in the wastebasket.'

'I'm afraid you're right.' He held the sheet to the light, squinted at it long and hard, wrote something into his book and then pocketed it. 'Watermark,' he explained. 'I can trace that paper easily, if I have to.'

Homer puffed his stogie heavily. From somewhere in the hall, a clock bonged six times. The big studio was quiet as the shadows behind the desk.

He moved silently to the easel, and I looked over his shoulder at the half-completed drawing in the frame. It was a typical magazine layout for an illustration. In the foreground, dominating the composition, sat the spineless figure of a dame, her long torso curving fluidly into nothingness. Her head was bent back so that readers might marvel at her swanlike neck. (All standard Shipley heroines sported the same snaky throats, too long for a normal woman or a normal jugular.) Her eyes were half closed, mysterious, heavy-lidded. Her mouth, full, half opened, inviting, was almost puckered with a waiting kiss for the broad-shouldered clothes horse who leaned over her, his long jaw almost at her chin.

Our hero, too, was stock Shipley art. Tall, muscular, small of face and large of collar, he looked for all the world like a Macy's window wax gigolo. (Could Nevin have posed for this?) His almost feminine lips curved in an inhuman smile. A lock of Wendell Willkie fluff fell casually over his high and unwrinkled forehead.

The illustration (had it been finished) would have been done in the hodgepodge technique that was the symbol of Shipley's talent. He had a knack for atmosphere. He finished his work with a combination of pencil, pen and ink, lampblack and the scrapings of *Conté* crayon, diligently rubbed into his backgrounds. His characters always moved against these backgrounds — masses of heavy shadow, a perfect device for hiding his unsound drawing.

For the drawing beneath the fog of Shipley's 'atmosphere' was tight, indeed. He had a few stock poses for his models, and he never varied them. But the editors never seemed to care. Did Shipley? I thought he had reached his peak five years ago. Only recently had I noticed a change — for the better. I wondered then whether Shipley meant to set a new goal for his art. Or was he content to sit on his mountain in Woodstock, satisfied with his glory, and happy with the four-figure checks that flew his way with every passing breeze?

Homer stood away from the easel, in the manner of a connoisseur.

'What do you think of this daub, Rembrandt?'

'It stinks!'

'I'm serious. Is it up to Shipley's standard?'

'What standard?'

Homer eyed me balefully.

'It stinks,' I repeated. 'That's my way of saying it's a Shipley original.'

'You artists are all alike — seething with professional jealousy. Why is that? If I were asked to examine a man's manuscript, I'm sure my judgment wouldn't be quite so severe — especially if he were a recognized professional.'

'How about *The Rover Boys*?'

'Stop quibbling,' said Homer. 'What's wrong with this picture? Why does it stink?'

'Simple, Homer. A trained eye can see the faults in a bad art job as quickly as you can taste garlic. Shipley violated all the laws. That, in itself, wouldn't have been so bad. But he covered his bad drawing with theatrical gauze atmosphere. He faked, Homer!'

'I wouldn't know about that.' Homer smiled faintly. 'But would you say that this is a recent Shipley? Is it typical of his latest work?'

I studied the sketch and tried to figure how much more Shipley might have done to the sketch.

'That's a tough one, Homer. I've never seen a Shipley illustration in the works before. Looks to me as though he had lots more to do on it.' I rubbed the surface of the board. 'I don't think this is a fresh sketch, at that. Could be a job he set up just to impress his weekend guests.'

'That's an interesting thought, Hank.'

He leaned into the easel, almost rubbing his nose on the illustration board. 'The paper seems a bit yellowed at the edges. Could that mean anything?'

I took the drawing off the board and felt the paper. It was the usual medium-priced type of sheet. I had used such stuff for many of my own masterpieces. But the edges were a bit yellowed, and bigshot artists don't usually submit finished work on old stock. Yellow paper would louse up a reproduction.

When I turned the board over, the brand name told me a story.

'Look here, Homer. This sheet is marked Bergot Fréres. Bergot Fréres was a French outfit selling this stock to American art stores about four years ago. Maybe before that. Anyhow, they went out of business four years ago.'

'Are you sure?'

'Yep. I remember that I tried to load up with some of the stuff at the time. It's good paper. But every art store in the city had sold out.'

Homer made a note of the brand name. 'I wonder whether Shipley stocked any more of this stuff in his cupboards. Maybe he bought up a supply of this stock and was still using it.'

'Here you are, Homer.' I eased out a few huge bundles of Bergot Fréres stock, still encased in their overseas wrappings. Homer slit them open. All were yellow with age.

'The guy must have had a hoarding mania,' I said. 'This paper's worthless.'

'Perhaps,' said Homer thoughtfully.

He squatted on the pile of paper and drew out his book again. The cigar slid into the corner of his mouth and made room for a rapt smile. He was a fat tailor, grinning over a tricky seam. No, he was a dwarf. He was Dopey, in a quiet moment.

I grabbed a slice of paper and made a record of my idea.

10

I Lean, Eileen

On the broad porch, the icy mountain breezes slapped my face and made me breathe again. It was a sharp evening. The snow flurries had long since disappeared over the mountain, leaving the moon master. The row of oaks beyond the road stood out against the silver disc like filigreed trees in a Russell Patterson landscape.

Sudden shadows moved near the Tucker place. I stepped beyond the edge of the porch for a better squint into the landscape. It was difficult to see that far. Was one shadow moving, or two? The black mass of shadow fell on a wall — the side of Tucker's house.

I ran into the studio for Homer. He sat where I had left him, like a fat Buddha. He raised only an eye when I ran in.

'I've just seen visitors down by the

Tuckers' place!' I puffed. 'Looked like a couple of 'em.'

Homer lifted his head slowly.

'Why shouldn't you? Any reason why the Tuckers shouldn't have visitors tonight?'

'In the snow?' I yapped. 'On the north side of the house?'

'That makes a difference!'

He lifted his fanny off the bundles. We skipped down the hall for our coats.

On the porch, Homer pulled me to a standstill, I followed his finger. There was a figure approaching from the direction of the woods to the southeast.

'Gavano!' Homer stepped spryly off the porch to cut him off.

Gavano seemed headed in the direction of the garage. We followed the footpath around the side of the house and waited for him to reach the driveway.

When he reached the driveway and stomped his feet on the hard snow, we stepped out.

'Out picking acorns, Mike?'

Gavano wheeled to face us, startled. I saw his right hand snap into his coat pocket, in a gangster gun grope.

The moon showed us his gilt smile. He answered Homer mockingly, both hands rammed into his coat, shoulders hunched. 'Nah. I been out counting the snowflakes, Bull.'

Homer stepped forward under Gavano's nose.

'Mike, I'm going to give you some advice.'

Gavano took a step toward the house, but Homer grabbed his elbow gently but firmly. The big man stopped, shaking off Homer's hand with a snarl.

Homer said: 'I'd advise you to keep away from the Tuckers' house, Mike.'

Gavano threw his head back and bellowed a horse laugh at the moon. It was an idiot's laugh, long and loud and rasping. The hills picked it up when Mike had finished, and the muffled echo goose-pimpled my shanks.

'That all you got to worry about, Bull?'

'I'm not worrying, Gavano.'

There was a touch of madness in their silhouettes. I moved in close, waiting for a fight that never came.

The rat eyes narrowed. 'Now Mike Gavano's giving you advice, Bull. Forget about me, see?'

He moved away up the driveway, hunched into his coat, an evil figure among the shadows.

Homer stared after him, rolling his stogie on his lip and still smiling. Then he turned and poked me in the ribs. 'Could it have been Gavano you saw a while ago?'

'I don't see how. I don't think he had time to make such a wide detour, if he were returning from Tuckers' place.'

'Simple enough to find out.'

And it was. Gavano had left two sets of footprints in the snow — the only footprints visible on our side of the clearing. I waded in with Homer.

The footsteps led into the woods bordering the small clearing and then turned sharp right along the stone wall. Homer paused to look back at the house. He pointed to the Tucker place, now half hidden beyond the hill.

'I think it's obvious why Gavano followed this wall to the top of the hill.'

'What in hell for?'

'To watch, Hank,' he led me on. 'Mike went over this way to get an unobstructed view of the area around Nat's backyard.'

We reached the end of the stone wall. Homer was right. The footprints ended at the wall and doubled back the way we had come.

'But what I don't understand, Homer — '

There was a sudden jerk, and I found myself behind a tree, held flat against the trunk by Homer's fat right arm. Laughter rose in my throat, for some unaccountable reason. But I swallowed my hysterics when he pointed. The silhouette of a man crunched through the snow at a half-run, in a beeline toward the garage.

'Want me to follow him?' I gulped.

Homer's grip tightened on my arm, while the figure disappeared over the hillock of snow. I turned to Homer impatiently — he was peering down the hill in the direction of Nat Tucker's place.

He faced me finally, calm as you please.

'Now, Hank, do exactly as I say. Hop back to the house as fast as you can — but not too fast. I don't want you to catch our mysterious snowbird. I don't want you to leap on him and beat him into a bloody pulp. I don't even want him to know you're following. Go to the garage and examine the place for footprints. When you've found them, hoof it back to Tucker's. I'll be waiting for you there.'

I wanted to ask him a few whys, but he had already stepped off down the hill. He turned his head and waved me away with a fat hand.

It was a good fifty yard dash from the wall to the driveway, and the spread eagle skid on my elbows added another ten to the distance. Plus time out for dusting the ice out of my nose. When I struggled to my feet, a figure had stepped from the shadows. It was Stanley Nevin.

'That was a nasty fall, MacAndrew.'

Was it the moonlight that made him zombie-colored? I made a mental note of the trick way the light promoted his high cheek bones.

'It's a great night for tripping and falling,' I said, by way of making chit-chat. 'There must be a half inch layer of ice on the driveway.'

'Much easier getting around on skis.' His eyes were fixed on a point somewhere far beyond my head, but only for a second. 'Ever try night skiing?'

I laughed. 'I can't even ski during the day, Nevin — I'd be the spirit of the pratt fall at night.'

There was a long pause.

Nevin said: 'It's getting too cold for comfort out here. Coming in?'

'Not yet. Think I'll practice falling; then maybe I won't lose so much elbow next time.'

He moved away toward the garage, while I lit a cigarette and stared at the stars. So it was Nevin we'd seen running through the snow. I wondered what he had been doing over at Nat's house. Why should he visit the Tuckers at this hour? Suddenly I remembered the cigarette butt and the ski trails. Eileen! Did it mean that he and Eileen had met up on the hill in the afternoon? Was this just another appointment with her? Hell — there was a moon and stars. I shivered.

My job was done. I edged slowly down

the driveway, lost in dreary speculation.

In Nat's living room Homer held a few sheets of typewritten stuff and leaned against the fireplace, turning a glass of ale in his hand. He greeted me before I could open my mouth.

'Well, Hank — glad you came down, finally. I looked all over for you before I left the house.'

There was ample time for me to catch his flickering wink.

'Changed my mind.' I forced a smile. 'Saw the light and figured I'd drop in.'

Eileen eyed me brightly from the kitchen door. 'I'm so glad you came, Hank. Would you like beer or ale? Or perhaps some whiskey?'

'I'm not much of a drinking man, Eileen. Maybe you'd better bring me all three.'

Eileen's girlish laughter made me feel good, in spite of Stanley Nevin. But why had she changed so suddenly? Her eyes were dulled with some emotion I couldn't understand. Was she afraid? No — it was worry, I decided. Eileen seemed worried. Why? I missed the apples in her cheeks, the usual brightness in her blue eyes. Hers was a magazine cover face — a face for the *American Magazine*, photographed by Bruehl, with a flower in her black hair and cobalt-blue satin laid against her skin.

Nat came in, rubbing his eyes. 'Well, this is a surprise, fellers. Glad to see you.'

Homer crossed the room to pump Nat's hand.

'Been napping, Nat?'

'Just about to,' he said, squinting from Homer to me. 'Cold weather makes a man sleepy, now don't it?'

Eileen must have reached the kitchen by way of the make-up kit, for her face had new color when she brought in the tray. Or was she only surprised to see her father in the room?

Homer thumbed the notes. 'This synopsis is very interesting, Eileen. It shows a remarkable memory for detail. Too bad you couldn't get to read the rest of Shipley's masterpiece — I mean the part he wrote in longhand.'

Eileen blushed prettily. 'It was really awfully easy. Aside from Mr. Shipley's disappointment in his friends, he mentioned only Mike Gavano. It's hard to forget a character like Mike — even in one chapter of a book.'

'You're being modest, Eileen. You've interpreted the mood of Shipley's writing for me — and you've done it very well.'

Tucker beamed at his daughter. 'Eileen's got talent, all right. Gets it from her maw — Mrs. Tucker was a keen one for business.' He winked. 'Long before ladies were supposed to have brains.'

Nat's eyes shifted from Eileen to Homer as he talked. He had that habit — a half dozen quick eye-rolls to each sentence. They were quick, birdlike glances, but accompanied by no movement of the head. Long ago there was a movie actor, character actor, who had used that optical gesture on the screen. Perhaps that was why I watched Nat with sudden interest.

'Eileen's got talent,' said Nat again, winking an eye.

'Nonsense, Father. I've done nothing remarkable.'

Tucker reddened to the ears. 'Indeed you have, girl!' He turned to Homer. 'You see, Bull, she's modest — downright humble, I might say!'

There was an embarrassing silence.

'Downright humble!' Nat mumbled. 'Trouble is this place — this consarned job of mine.'

'Oh, Dad, *please!*'

''Tain't your fault, at that, Eileen. A woman gets to feelin' meek and simple, livin' like we do — like servants.'

A flicker of annoyance clouded Eileen's eyes.

Homer said: 'Nonsense, Nat. There's nothing wrong with being a caretaker. Nothing at all.'

'Of course not,' I echoed. 'Taking care of a place like this is a responsible job.'

'Pah,' snapped Nat bitterly. 'It's being a servant! Never thought I'd feel like a common servant. Never thought I'd have to raise my girl this way.'

Eileen went to him and lifted his head. 'You know I'm perfectly happy, Dad.'

He looked at her mournfully. 'You're a brave girl, Eileen.'

'Nothing of the sort. I'm perfectly happy — do you understand? Happy with our home and your job and — everything. Oh, if you'd only believe me, Dad. Why, we haven't a worry in the world, have we?'

Tucker stared at his pipe. It seemed odd for a man with so homespun a pan to harbor such ideas. You walk through a village full of Nat Tuckers — farmers, store-keepers, real estate agents, hotel keepers. You've seen his face, thousands of times. It's a usual face, a face to forget, an upstate face no different from all the others. You say: 'Tucker? An honest farmer, brought up in the hills. Inherited his father's farm, worries about nothing more serious than the mortgage.' There are a million Tuckers in every state in the union. You see him over and over again. In the fields. Behind a counter. Tucker is always a bit player in a simple scene, unimportant and vague.

I wondered what lay behind this Tucker's eyes.

He shook his head and smiled weakly at his daughter. 'I'm sorry, Eileen.'

She brought him a glass of ale, and he sipped it dreamily.

Homer said: 'Do you mind a few more questions, Eileen?'

'Fire away,' she said brightly.

'When you went up to your work at the house, did you talk to anybody much, other than Shipley?'

'I guess I talked to all of them, at one time or another.'

'Did you meet Miss Deming before you went up on Friday?'

'Only on the hill, once or twice, when I'd go out to ski.'

'Talk to her much?'

Eileen nodded. 'Mr. Shipley introduced us. She was very nice to me — at first.'

'At first?'

Eileen paused to wrinkle her nose. 'I mean before I started to work for Mr. Shipley.'

'You mean that she was unpleasant?'

'Not exactly. Outwardly, she seemed as pleasant as usual. But I felt ill at ease, in spite of her honeyed words. It seemed to me that Miss Deming didn't want me up at the house. She questioned me interminably about my experience. She warned me about Mr. Shipley's 'eccentricities,' and cautioned me against mentioning my job to any of the guests. It seemed to me that she was worried about something.'

'The book?'

'Perhaps. She did suggest, once, that I leave all of my finished typing with her.'

'Now we're getting somewhere,' said Homer. 'Did you do as she suggested?'

'I couldn't, and I had to tell her the reason. You see, Mr. Shipley told me to show the notes to nobody — under any circumstances. I mentioned Miss Deming's instructions, and I remember that he frowned and said: 'Include Miss B out!'' Eileen blushed. 'That was the first and last time Mr. Shipley used profanity in my presence. He must have seen that I didn't like that sort of talk, for he apologized gracefully.'

'What did Miss Deming say when you told her about Shipley's orders?'

Eileen smiled. 'There was a scene, of course, and from that day on, her dislike for me was quite apparent.'

'What about Shipley?'

'How do you mean?'

'When you worked with him, did he seem worried?'

'I don't know, exactly. Most of my

impressions of him are based on nothing more than his manner as he dictated to me. He seemed in a great hurry to get started with that book, and sometimes became angry with himself because of his inexperience with that sort of thing.'

'Did Miss Deming ever come into the studio while he was dictating?'

'She came in on Friday morning. Of course, he stopped dictating immediately. She wanted to talk to him about the weekend guests. It seemed that he hadn't told her how many were coming up and she didn't know how to instruct the cook. Mr. Shipley's manner changed noticeably when she asked him about the weekend party. He became irritable, impatient and — well, nervous while they talked about the party.'

'Nervous?'

Eileen groped for the right word. 'If not nervous, at least concerned, or worried, perhaps. He wondered whether *all* the guests would come, and they mentioned a few of the people expected.'

Homer leaned forward. 'Remember any of that?'

'I'm sorry that I don't. But, you see, all these names were strange to me. And then again, Miss Deming made me fidgety whenever I saw her. It wasn't easy for me when she was around.'

'I understand,' said Homer.

'Me, too,' I added. 'That dame gives me the screaming meemies!'

'Shipley didn't mention my name, did he?' Homer asked.

'He might have,' she said. 'I honestly can't remember.'

Homer flipped another page in his little black book. 'Can you tell me who arrived first, Eileen?'

'Cunningham and Trum. They arrived on Friday afternoon, and Miss Deming brought them into the studio while I was there. Mr. Shipley dismissed me as soon as they walked in.'

'Did you see them much after that? I mean — to talk?'

'Mr. Cunningham spoke to me at great length later in the day. He was out skiing and stopped to chat on the porch. He seemed interested in my work.'

'You mean the book, of course?'

She nodded. 'I'm afraid that Mr. Cunningham was trying to pump me.' Eileen laughed. 'Isn't that what you detectives call it?'

'That's what it sounds like,' I chirped, feeling like Nero Wolfe.

'Can you remember a few of his questions?'

'I remember one, very clearly. He asked: 'Is it a *funny* book?' Then he explained that Mr. Shipley was a very funny fellow at times. Of course, I told him nothing.'

'Did he try again?'

'Oh, yes, several times.'

Homer was taking his notes in shorthand again. 'How about Trum?'

'I think Mr. Trum is cute. He reminds me of Guy Kibbee — sort of fat and harmless. He was always very pleasant to me.'

'Was he interested in the book, too?'

'Casually. He would ask things like, 'How's the epic coming, Eileen?' or 'Is your face red from all the scandal?' Perhaps he was looking for information, too. But he really never had a chance to speak to me alone, you see. Miss Lawrence was usually with him — or Cunningham.'

Homer's manner didn't change at the mention of Grace. 'Did Miss Lawrence arrive with Cunningham and Trum?'

'No. I remember her big yellow roadster came up the driveway about six o'clock on Friday evening. I was in the kitchen preparing dinner when she drove through.'

'Have any contact with the lady?'

'I like Grace. It's a funny thing about her — in many ways she's like Miss Deming. I mean that she seems hard-boiled. She's much nicer than Miss Deming, though. Warmer.'

Homer enjoyed the backhanded praise of his ex-wife. 'I suppose she, too, was interested in the book?'

'Grace?' Eileen asked herself. 'I don't think so. As a matter of fact, I'd say that she was the only guest completely *disinterested* in the book. The others made a point of trying to wheedle information out of me.'

'Let's see,' said Homer. 'We have only

Nicky English, Gavano and Nevin left to talk about. I haven't any doubt but that Nicky made a point of annoying you. Am I right?'

'Indeed you are. Nicky English is the sort of man who makes an impression right away — probably because of the way he dresses. But my memory of Nicky would be pretty vivid anyhow. You see, he came into the studio as soon as he arrived, even before he'd taken off his overcoat.'

'That was on Friday evening then?'

'At about eighty-thirty. I should say he ran into the studio. He always seemed to be running, somehow. Anyway, when he met Mr. Shipley in the studio, I thought him rather rude. I thought there would be a scene for a minute — he was that rude. But Mr. Shipley seemed to enjoy the way Nicky carried on. Nicky said something like: 'What's the gag, Shipley? Why the invite?' But that was all I heard. Mr. Shipley asked me to leave after that.'

'Eileen,' said Homer, 'you're doing swell. What else did you see of Nicky English?'

'Plenty. Of all the people in the house, Nicky was the most brazen about the book. He cornered me several times and he wasn't even subtle.'

'That's a laugh,' I said. 'He's a master of innuendo in the public press.'

'He may write that way,' she said evenly. 'But it seemed to me that he was really trying to talk business whenever he ran into me. I almost expected him to make me an offer for my shorthand notes on Friday night.'

'But he never did, actually?'

'No — unless I wasn't bright enough to understand him.'

Eileen was modest. How could a woman be so pretty and that smart? You read about people like Eileen in books, but do you meet them in gin mills? I made a resolution.

'We can forego Gavano and Nevin, for the present,' said Homer. He flipped shut his little black book.

The interview was over.

'Look at Dad,' whispered Eileen. 'We've put him to sleep.'

And so we had. Nat Tucker slumped

forward in his rocker, whistling gently through his grey mustache. Homer nudged my middle, and we edged to the door.

'Good night,' she cooed. And then: 'Good night, Hank.' She gave me her nicest smile, as though she might stay.

'Good night,' I murmured. 'See you later.'

When I looked back, she was at the window, waving me another goodbye.

11

I'm Dizzy, Homer

The moon had gone to bed in a blanket of cirrostratus, but the night still glowed with an eerie light. It was grey and cold and quiet. Homer was thinking overtime, and I — my mind was full of Eileen and Nevin and a hundred unanswered questions.

'Well, sonny,' Homer began finally, 'did you follow our mystery man to his lair?'

'It was easy,' I explained. 'The mystery man was Nevin.'

Homer stopped walking, he was that stunned. 'Impossible!'

I described the incident at the garage.

'I see,' Homer mumbled. 'Then you didn't examine the garage for footprints?'

'What for? When I saw Nevin I put two and two together.'

'And got zero! How can you be sure that Nevin was our man?'

That stopped me. I couldn't be sure.

'Did you notice his pants?' Homer asked. 'The snow is over six inches deep — it would have left his pants white at the cuffs.'

I shook my head woefully.

'No matter.'

We started through the snow in the direction of the hillock where Mr. Mystery had begun his fifty-yard sprint. When we reached the trail of footsteps, Homer paused to squint back at the Tuckers' house.

'Just as I thought,' he said. 'Our man came from Nat Tucker's backyard.'

'I don't get it, Homer. What would Nevin want back there?'

'Not so fast. Placing Nevin in Nat's back yard is your idea.'

'You don't think it was Nevin?'

'I know it wasn't Nevin!' Homer beamed up at me.

I groaned. 'All right. MacAndrew is a moron. Who was it?'

'MacAndrew is no such animal,' he said. 'MacAndrew is only an artist who hasn't learned to use his eyes.'

We crunched through the snow. I was floored. I could remember only a running silhouette, a hill, a vague background of moonlit sky. I tried to light up the dark corners in my brain. But the switch was broken. I couldn't remember.

'Notice anything peculiar about our scurrying silhouette?'

He was putting it very plainly. I hung my head and fought for an idea.

'Wasn't he short?'

Somewhere in the dark depths of my head, a small light went on. Fifteen volts, no more, no less. 'I'd say he was,' I said.

'How many shorties in our cosy house party up yonder?'

That was easy. 'Two.'

'Exactly. Trum and Nicky English.'

An additional thirty watts clicked on.

'Nat Tucker's short, too,' I added.

'We can forget Nat. But how does Trum dress, Hank?'

'Like a cigarette tycoon, I guess.'

'From here on in, it's a breeze,' laughed Homer. 'Trum is short and fat. He couldn't make that fifty yards in anything under two minutes — through snow. Our man made it in almost nothing flat. He lifted his legs high. He was light on his feet. He wore a flared coat — an Esquire model, probably. Our prowler then — '

'Nicky English!' I chirped.

'Of course.'

'But what's the gag? Why was Nicky coming from Nat's?'

We reached the driveway. Homer stomped the snow off his shoes and flicked at his trousers.

'Your guess is as good as mine.'

My guess was worthless. I imagined that Nicky made the trip to try to buy the new notes from Eileen. It was a stupid idea — unfit to mention.

We strolled to the garage. Homer examined the floor for snow-marks. There were plenty. Nevin and Nicky and Gavano and a herd of wild horses might have stamped through that garage in the last hour. We entered the kitchen through the garage. It was empty.

So was the library. Homer locked the door and tossed Eileen's notes on the long table. 'Care to read your girlfriend's typing?'

'I'll read anything,' I said, 'if I can sit

still for fifteen minutes.'

Homer pulled the cord for Lester. 'I'll arrange it, sonny. But put those notes into your pocket until Lester leaves, will you?'

'You make me feel like the maiden in a Karloff thriller,' I said. 'Why the hush-hush?'

But Homer was serious. 'When I leave with Lester, you'll lock yourself in here, Hank. And don't open the door for anybody until I return. I'll be in the studio — I want to ask Lester a question or two about that easel.'

'What's the gag?' I grumbled. 'Why do I sit here and play hard to get?'

Homer stared at me impishly. 'I'm not thinking of you, Hank. It's those notes I value. I have a vague feeling that somebody may try to lay hands on them.'

'That'd be fun. Why not give 'em the chance? I'd like nothing better than to crack a few skulls before we leave this joint.'

There was a soft knock at the door.

'Do as I say,' cautioned Homer, and he opened the door for Lester. The big goon blinked at us. 'How long have you been in your room, Lester?'

'An hour, I guess.'

'Was your wife with you all that time?'

Lester nodded dumbly.

'Good,' said Homer. 'Tell me, Lester — how often did you clean Mr. Shipley's studio?'

'Every night.'

'Come with me.' Homer led him into the hall and I locked the door.

I relaxed in my fat chair, like a man in a furniture ad. It felt good to rest my bones. You get into a room lined with books and something happens to your inner man, somehow. Now I lit a cigarette and turned to Eileen's notes.

I read on:

MEMORY NOTES — CHAPTER ONE OF MR. SHIPLEY'S MANUSCRIPT: *(I'm using the first person, as Mr. Shipley did throughout this chapter. I thought that by doing the notes this way, I could give you a clearer picture of what was written.)*

'This is a dirty book about dirty people!'

So, my friends, beware! I am tired of friends, bored with friends, deceived by friends, betrayed by friends, attacked by friends, etc., etc. (*In the manner of a tirade by Balzac.*) I have too many friends and not enough enemies. Why? Because all of my friends are my hypothetical enemies. I'd rather have a villain marked than hidden in the soft soap of a meaningless and artificial camaraderie. Enemies strike in the open. A man has a chance to draw his gun and return the fire. Friends? Friends connive, betray subtly, kill slowly, etc. Paradox of paradoxes — my friendly enemies must remain so — but for how long? I had a friend once. Now even he is gone. Or are you gone, Mike Gavano? (*Here, a long passage explaining the fact that Gavano was once his boyhood pal. They were brought up together in the slums of New York's East Side. He describes the tenement, the poverty, his family and the struggle for existence. He describes the East Side as 'the black cesspool of the biggest city in the world. 'He goes on to say that he would still be in that part of the world if it weren't for Mike Gavano.)* Mike and I were pals. Mike was a big kid — hard and tough and fearless. I have always been a coward. Once Mike saved my life. He taught me to know that I was a coward; that I wasn't built for the life I had fallen into. I wasn't a criminal. I couldn't steal. Danger made me tremble with fear. Mike did me a great service. He proved to me that I was a coward. Because of him, I quit the group of misfits. I began to study — to sketch — to go to school. Mike made me an artist. But, Mike, I apologize. I can't forget that night when we met, years later. I didn't shake your hand. I didn't want to know you, Mike Gavano. It would have seemed strange to my friends if I had said hello.

I am apologizing to you, Mike. I dropped your hand like a hot coal. I snubbed you. Now you want me to be sorry for the rest of my life, don't you, Mike? You know how much of a coward I am. You think I'm afraid to talk. This book is yours, too, Mike. Read it and you will see why. I'm dedicating it to you first, Mike Gavano. And after you?

It was after this last paragraph that I dozed off. Maybe it was the first bottle of stout I had gulped at Nat's. Maybe I was tired. Or it might have been that Shipley's reference to Gavano didn't shock me. Plenty of artists have worked their way up from cesspools.

I awoke to the sound of thumping on the library door. Not thumping — pounding. It frightened me for a minute. The door was actually trembling under the violent fists of somebody or other. For another minute I thought that the notes might be gone. I was clutching them in my right hand.

I grabbed the yellow volume of erotica from the shelf, slapped the pages shut on the notes and returned it to its place among the books.

Should I unlock the door? Homer's warning checked me.

'What do you want?' I managed.

'It's Lester! Open up!'

I stepped toward the door and paused.

'What's up? What do you want?'

'It's Mr. Bull — he's been slugged in the studio!'

I swung the door open and held the knob in my hand. Lester stood before me. His face was a mask of fright. All the high-blood-pressure pink had left his cheeks, and his eyes were wide with horror.

'You were in there with him, you ape! What happened?' I grabbed him by the lapels and tried to shake.

'I went out. I dunno — '

I pushed him backward an inch and sprinted down the hall before he could finish. My heart did nip-ups around my larynx.

I heard Lester puffing behind me as I ran.

12

Sluggings in the Studio

I felt my heart beat a tattoo against my ribs.

It was horrible.

Homer lay on his back, near the huge oak easel. A crimson stream was curving a path down his fat cheek to the rug. The sight of the dripping blood stabbed at my midriff and made me swallow by breath. Under that blood, Homer's face was the color of the unwashed dead, pale and grey and unlovely to look at. I forced myself to bend over his chest. There was the slow rhythm of breathing.

'What happened to the lights?' I yapped at Lester over my shoulder. 'Who turned off the lights?'

'I dunno,' he drooled. 'He was standing in the hall when I left him. I didn't see no lights on in here.'

I got off my knees and shoved the goon

on his way. He muttered and minced out of the room.

There was a sink arrangement in the far corner of the studio that Shipley must have used for his artwork. I found an old towel and small bowl in the tabouret and filled the bowl in the sink.

I kneeled at Homer's side. The cold water brought a flicker to his eyes and he stirred a bit. I wet the towel again and wiped away the grisly stain on his cheek. He had been hit hard, right over the forehead.

I bent to lift him on the couch when something hard and heavy thwacked down on my head. The grey mass that was the couch became a fiery torch that rose up to slap me in the face. A flash of pain stabbed at my head and whirled me around in a world of technicolored stars and stripes. I felt myself spin off into a bottomless pit, red and green and yellow lights flashing in my brain.

★　★　★

Someone had slapped a ragful of ice on my head. Ice water, stinking from some antiseptic, trickled down my nose, splashed on my chin and drooled off down my neck. An eight-cylinder engine banged rhythmically in my brain, and from somewhere up over my forehead I felt nine thousand needles prick my scalp.

I opened my eyes. A strange blurred face peered down at me. He came into focus after a second and I knew he must be the doctor Lester had called.

Homer, his own head festooned in a mess of bandage, stared at me smilingly from over the medico's shoulder.

'Take it easy, son,' said the doctor. 'You've had a bad shock.'

'What hit me?' I asked, trying to get up.

The doctor eased me down into the pillows. 'Don't get up until you feel strong enough.'

I heard Swink cluck in Homer's ear. 'He's hit bad.'

'What hit me, Homer?'

Homer shoved a wicked-looking fireplace tool under my nose. 'You walked into this, Hank. A blunt instrument,' he added with a smile, 'wielded with great force.'

I sat up. The room began to surround me, move away and then spin around at an obtuse angle.

'Be careful now, sonny,' said Homer.

I made it. I was on the leather davenport in the studio. A crowd of shadowy heads came into focus, and I saw Grace and Trum whispering near the window. Cunningham gaped at me from the end of the davenport, shaking his head sadly. Behind Homer stood Olympe, her hands full of bandage, her oval face pale and frightened. Stanley Nevin stood beside her, almost as pale.

'No fracture, Doc?' asked Homer. 'This iron is heavy enough to kill a man.'

The doctor touched my head gently. I squirmed. He said: 'You're both lucky, gentlemen. Lucky to be alive. Another inch to the right and we'd have a different story.'

I hefted the poker. 'Lucky for us we're natural fatheads, eh, Homer?' I tried to smile, but the needles jabbed deep into my sense of humor.

Swink said: 'Did you see anything before you were hit, MacAndrew?'

160

'Not before — after,' I corrected. 'I saw lots of funny lights.' I explained what had happened.

Homer called Lester over to the davenport. The big ape crossed the room all atwitter, fumbling his hands.

'Let's have it,' said Homer. 'From the time you left me in the hall.'

Lester cleared his throat. 'I was walkin' down to the kitchen, after leavin' you in the hall. My wife told me she wanted to give the food order, like she does every night this time. That's on account of I always phone the market for tomorrow's stuff. She was in the kitchen. She gives me the order and I start back to the phone in the main hall. I happen to look in the studio. Then I see you on the floor and run for Mr. MacAndrew.'

'You saw me from the hall?'

Lester fidgeted. 'No. I can't see you from the hall. I didn't hear nobody inside the studio, so I decide to take a look inside.'

'What made you look inside?'

'I dunno. Maybe it's because I think you're in here and there ain't any light on.'

161

'Did you turn the light on when you walked in?'

'No, I didn't.'

'Why not, if you were worried about me?'

'I dunno. I guess my eyes got used to seeing with only the hall light comin' in.'

'What did you do after you saw me?'

There was a pause. 'I was scared. I ran after Mr. MacAndrew right away.'

'Did you see anybody else in this room?' Homer snapped.

'Nobody.'

'What happened after Mr. MacAndrew came in here?'

'He told me to call a doc. I went to the hall phone and tried to get Doc Hilton. When I come back, there's Mr. Mac-Andrew, layin' on the floor with you.'

'Did you see anybody in the hall, after you made the phone call?'

Lester shifted, uneasily. 'I saw Mr. Cunningham. He was walking through the dining room.'

All eyes were on Cunningham.

Homer continued: 'How long were you gone to make that phone call?'

'It took time. I couldn't get the Doc right away.'

'That's true,' the doctor explained. 'My wife wasn't at home tonight. The maid gave Lester two phone numbers. Of course,' he said with a smile, 'I was at the second place.'

'Thank you, Doctor,' said Homer. 'That'll be all, Lester.'

Cunningham came forward. 'I suppose you'll be wanting to know what I was doing?'

'Not at all.' Homer beamed. 'What makes you think I'm interested?'

'You probably will be, sooner or later,' Cunningham said. 'I'd just come in from outside, through the kitchen. You can check on me with Minnie Minton.'

'Good enough, Cunningham.' Homer touched his head gingerly. 'Now, if you'll all kindly leave us alone — '

At that moment Nicky English entered the room, bedecked in a purple robe much too long for his boyish figure. He squinted around the studio in his birdlike fashion and his mouth dropped open in grinning amazement.

'What goes on?' he piped. 'Sherlock and Watson get socked by mysterious assailant?'

'Yeah,' I muttered. 'What detectives on what case were playfully conked by which mysterious thug in whose studio?' My gag got a laugh, but it didn't last long.

Homer eyed English slyly. 'Where were you when the light went out, Nicky?'

'Keep your shirt on, Bull; Nicky English is a past master at alibis.'

'Nicky English had better come up with a good one,' I muttered.

His lip curled my way. 'I was up in my room, Watson, preparing for my evening milk bath. I came down to bawl the hell out of Lester for filling my tub with Grade B. I am strictly a Grade A milk bather.'

'Very funny,' I shot. 'You should've been in vaudeville, Nicky. Vaudeville's as dead as your wisecracks.'

'I was in my room, Bull,' he snapped. 'Take it or leave it!'

'Don't be self-conscious, Nicky,' cooed Homer. 'Of course I'll take it. All newspaper men are intrinsically honest, aren't they?' He reached over and grabbed Nicky's hands suddenly. 'Are you anemic, Nicky? Or just cold? Your hands are like ice. One would think you'd just come back from another walk in the snow.'

English jerked his hands away. 'You're nuts. I just took a cold shower.'

Homer's face fell in mock agony. 'Of course, Nicky, of course. I forgot that you were the cold water type. Nothing like a cold shower before hitting the hay, eh?'

Gavano walked in, blowing on his hands.

Homer chuckled. 'You just have a cold shower, too, Mike?'

Gavano gaped at our bandages, then laughed out loud. 'I'll be damned! Somebody beat me to it, Bull!' He pointed to me and burst into a fresh spasm. 'I could'a done better myself!'

'You think this is an amateur job, Gavano?'

Gavano nodded violently. 'O' course! I don't hit nobody behind his back. See, I woulda smashed your little schnozzle into a pulp, Bull!'

'In that case, I'll be a Pollyanna,' said

Homer, and he fingered his bandages lightly. 'Now, if you people will all be good enough to leave, MacAndrew and I would appreciate a few moments of solitude.'

Swink showed them out. I saw Trum hesitate at the door. He came over to the davenport.

'I'd like to speak to you for a moment, if I may, Bull.'

Homer again held his head. 'I'm sorry, Trum. It'll have to wait.'

'But this is important.'

'I'll talk about it later. We must have time to lick our wounds.'

Trum sucked his lip and moved toward the door. 'I'll be waiting for you in my room, Bull.'

Homer dropped into an easy chair and fixed me with a cheery grin and a bleary eye. 'Feel any better?'

I nodded. 'Strong enough to go five rounds with the guy who slammed me. Now why would anyone want to slug innocent MacAndrew?'

'Look through your pockets, sonny. I expect our muscular friend has relieved you of Eileen's notes.'

'In a pig's eye, he did!'

'You mean you have them?'

'Definitely!' I said, and told him what had happened in the library, mentioning the name of the book I had cached them in, its location on the shelf and the color of the binding.

'Incredible! That loses you your amateur standing, Hank. Watson was a bungler compared to you.'

The pain in my head became a dull drum beat, and I eased down to a more comfortable position. Skittering sharp jabs ran up and down my spine. I could hear a few low voices from somewhere down the hall, but when I twisted my neck to catch them, the needles stabbed my head back into the pillows. I held my temples and said 'Damn it!' and bent forward until the pain passed.

For some reason or other, a sudden feeling of fear gnawed at my brain. Suppose the man with the poker came back again, switched out the main light and lit into me? I closed my eyes and toyed with the idea. I was certainly in bad shape for another such attack. There was sweat on my forehead.

I didn't like the idea. I forced my eyes open.

Grace Lawrence was standing at the end of the davenport, staring down at me. 'Oh, Hank,' she said, 'isn't this terrible? Was Homer hurt badly?'

'He'll live.'

She bit her lip.

'What's eating you, Grace?'

'What a louse I am!'

'Are you telling me, or asking me?'

She turned her wet eyes on me. 'Please, Hank, I didn't come back to wisecrack. I thought . . . '

She meant it. I patted her knee. 'MacAndrew apologizes, Grace. What's on your mind?'

'It's all this — this mess.' She bit her lip again and almost sobbed. 'I could have — '

I caught the sound of a step in the doorway.

It was Trum. He barged into the room, torn between a scowl and a frown. 'Ah, there you are, Grace.'

Grace wiped her eyes quickly and forced a laugh. 'Hello, honey — where on earth have you been?'

Trum eyed me with ice. 'I thought you were going to your room, Grace.'

'I came back for my cigarette case,' she breezed, patting a small evening bag. 'You worried about me, honey?'

'I wanted to speak to you,' he said. 'Are you finished with MacAndrew?'

'Why, Duggie,' she cooed, 'Mr. Mac-Andrew and I were only talking about — '

'Your portrait?' he snapped.

'But of course!' said Grace, slipping her arm around his.

I tried to scratch the purpose of Grace's visit out of my scalp. All I got was dandruff. What could she know? Had she seen the slugger crack me with the poker? Something must have happened to Grace that hit her hard — hard enough to break down her native nonchalance — her icy indifference to Homer and me and all the warmer virtues. Thinking made my head heave.

And while I meditated, Homer bounced in.

'Drunk again, Hank? Or just back to normal?'

'I'm as weak as a canary,' I gulped. 'But MacAndrew's canaries live on Bourbon.'

'Pour one for another canary.'

I poured one. 'Did you get the notes?'

'No,' he said simply.

I dropped another pint on the rug, and Homer rescued the bottle.

'The notes are gone, sonny. And so is your favorite book of pornography.'

'I'll be damned!' I muttered, resting my amazement against the cupboard. 'I don't care about those notes — but the dirty crook swiped my book!'

Homer finished his glass in one full gulp, which was Homer's way of saying the liquor was good. He shrugged. 'It's just as well this way. Just as well.'

'What do you mean?'

'Did you read the notes?'

I nodded. 'They read like the introduction to a biography of Mike Gavano.'

Homer refilled his glass and squatted, sighing. 'Exactly. And we don't need Mike Gavano's biography. We can get it in the Brooklyn police records whenever we need it, Hank. What puzzles me is why anybody should slug us for — ' He broke off at the faint sound of a telephone in the next room. They heard Swink answer it. Homer said: 'I'll bet that's the Shtunk . . . let's go see.'

13

Monologue by the Shtunk

Jesse Swink handed Homer the telephone.

'Feller named Smith askin' for you,' he explained. 'Sounds tight as a drum.'

Homer held a hand over the mouthpiece. 'Any extensions upstairs, Swink?'

'There's one up in the main hall.'

Homer nodded me toward the stairs. 'Let's keep this a person to person call, Hank.'

Upstairs, the phone sat on a little table near the right-angle hallway that led to the attic. There was a small bay window neatly decorated with rust-colored drapes. A long medieval chest lay under the windows, its broad sides overflowing with rococo scrawls and carvings. I pulled up a spindly chair and grabbed the phone.

'Okay, Homer,' I said.

'Go ahead, Shtunk,' said Homer. 'Did

172

you get anything?'

'All day long I been on my pins,' nasaled the Shtunk. 'I got plenty to tell Mr. Bull.'

There was a silence.

'Spill it, Shtunk!'

'Excuse me, I am just swallowing my sandwich. I am in a bar — The White Horse.'

Homer snorted. 'I don't care where you are. Talk fast — this is a toll call!'

'Haw!! Haw! No it ain't, Mr. Bull. Like I was saying, I am eating a sandwich in this White Horse place. It is up here, I am up here.'

'He's drunk!' I said.

'Up *where*?' Homer moaned.

'I am in this White Horse place, in Kingston.'

I found Homer buzzing with Swink in the hall.

'Mind if I come along, Bull?'

Homer wriggled into his coat. 'Why not? I think you'll find my friend Mr. Smith interesting, and you can guide me to an address I must find tonight.' He fumbled in his pockets and produced one of the bills from Shipley's desk. 'Know a Doctor Torrance?'

'Indeed I do! But I don't think you'll find old Torrance in, Bull.' Swink massaged his jaw dubiously. 'I think he's away to Miami this time of year.'

'Too bad. Is his office in town?'

I swung the car through the main gate, and we rolled and bumped down the rutty road.

Swink said: 'Not quite. I guess Torrance's still a country doctor at heart. He's a poke out of town, Bull.'

'Anybody in the house?'

'Well, now — ' Swink eyed Homer curiously. ' — I don't rightly know. What in blazes you want with Torrance?'

'Just a straw. I wonder could we — ah — get into the doctor's house, Swink?'

'Now?'

'Why not? It'd only take me a minute to get what I want.'

'And what might that be?'

There was a long silence.

'A card, Swink. It might be everything — and nothing. Was Torrance a New York doctor originally?'

'Up until a few years ago. Famous old gent, he was. He came back to Kingston to retire, but he still has a few patients. Down in New York, Torrance was a big man — one of the biggest, they tell me. But he got fed up with them fancy patients of his — decided to retire up here in the place where he was born.'

I tried to put the information in an important place — to weave it into the chain of events. I failed.

'You think Shipley went to this old duck when he was in the city, Homer?'

'Possibly. I could find out if we — ah — could get into his home for a few minutes.'

We rode on in silence until the last curve into Kingston.

'That there's old Torrance's place. Now.'

He pointed to the left of the road where a huge colonial house spread itself among the big pines.

'Nice low windows,' whispered Homer. 'My size.'

I smiled.

'Eh?' asked Swink.

'I was suggesting that MacAndrew slow

down in town,' Homer said brightly. 'We don't want to miss this White Horse Tavern.'

That was impossible. The White Horse Tavern, festooned in orange and green neon, was neither White nor a Tavern. It was a dog cart set back from the main street and surrounded by filling stations and the dribs and drabs of railroad station hostelry.

The Shtunk sat gloomily in the rear, fondling the last gulp in a glass of beer and munching pretzels.

Homer nodded. 'Let's see the stuff, Shtunk.'

'There ain't nothing to see, Mr. Bull,' whined the Shtunk. 'This pal of yours Gurney, on this newspaper, he is a stumblebum. He does not allow me to take no clippings. I must read them clippings and remember them, he says. That is why I have come up to Kingston, Mr. Bull. There is so much in my conk, I am afraid I will forget it unless I lam up here and spill quick.'

'You got something from Gurney's morgue, then?'

The waiter doled out the drinks. The Shtunk swallowed a long pull at the glass.

'Plenty. I start in with Nicky English. In Gurney's dump I find that English is no news up until he is big-time. That is the time he is beginning this column of his — this *Nicky's New York* corn. Then I see him a lot in this clip file of Gurney's. But it is not on account of English only. It is on account of this doll he is going around with steady.'

'Which doll?'

'This Marie Parrish dame. There is all kinds of fancy talk. They are keeping company. They are getting married. Gurney has plenty of snaps of them both.' He blew a kiss to the rafters. 'This Parrish doll is a looker.'

'I seem to remember the name,' said Homer. 'She was a chorus girl, wasn't she?'

'She was strictly Ziegfeld stuff.'

'She married him finally?'

'No, she does not marry the guy. I forget about her. But then a funny thing happens, when I'm starting on the clips about Trum.'

Homer interrupted. 'No more on English?'

The Shtunk shook his head. 'That is all I find on English, just this stuff about him going steady with the Parrish dame. But, like I say, I see more about her when I go into the Trum clips.'

He waited until Homer looked up from his little black book.

'This Trum guy is a funny duck. They got all kinds of stuff on him. I wade through a stack of pictures and junk for over an hour. It is mostly about his wives. The guy is lousy with wives — he had all kinds. Anyhow, I pass up all this. It is giving me a pain in the dome just looking at the headlines about this Trum.' He held his head. 'They have all kinds of pictures. I see his house, his nags, his boat, his plane. I'm ready to give up, when I find something that makes me sit up and take notice. It is this Parrish dame. She has been killed!'

'Of course!' snapped Homer. 'I remember the case now. Wasn't she the woman who was drowned on somebody's yacht back in '32?'

'On the nose,' said the Shtunk. 'But the boat belong to Trum! That is what gets me, Mr. Bull.'

Homer poked him in the ribs. 'That's worth another drink, Shtunk!'

'That is nothing, Mr. Bull.' He blinked. 'What I got next is better, even.' He paused dramatically, grinning around the table. 'There is a big smell in the papers, but it don't last. The clip file shows me only three days on the case. Then it is hushed.'

'How did she drown?'

'It is all a blank. Nobody knows. There is a big story about suicide.'

'Was Nicky on the boat?'

'There ain't a mention of English. But I see another guy on the boat. You know who I see?'

He waited until the waiter had gone.

'Who?' asked Homer.

'I see Shipley!'

'Are you sure? Are you sure it was Hugo Shipley?'

The Shtunk looked hurt. 'It is Hugo Shipley, I say. The clip mentions this fact. It says the guy is an artist. It says his name is *Shipley* — *Hugo Shipley*!'

I said: 'He's right, Homer. I remember the story. It always mystified me — I mean the way a heel illustrator like Shipley mixed with big business on yachts and things.'

Homer was delighted. 'Anybody else we know on that boat?'

'Yeah. Cunningham.'

Homer whistled tunelessly through his teeth.

'Cunningham is on with his wife, but they only rate a line. Most of the stuff is on Trum. Trum is heart-broke on account of this. Trum is going to sell his yacht. Trum is a nervous wreck. That is the last clip I see.'

'Did you check other files for the story?'

'I go back to Gurney. I ask for more, on account of I know it is important. Gurney sniffs. He says: 'That stink was a phoney. The story died after three days. It smelled like a fix at the time, on account of Trum's dough.' There is no more dope, even in the front page stuff Gurney pulls out for me.'

Swink shook his head. 'I don't get it, Bull. What in tarnation you trying to prove?'

'I sent the Shtunk out to ferret information,' said Homer. 'That was because there seemed to be something incongruous about the guests at this last weekend party.'

'But that stuff's all dead.'

'I wonder. Unfinished police cases have always interested me, Swink. There's usually a pretty good reason for whitewash.'

'That's what I don't see,' Swink said. 'You don't believe the woman was drowned?'

Homer smiled patiently. 'I must believe she drowned. But could she swim?'

The Shtunk broke in. 'The doll can't swim, Mr. Bull. It is in the clip that she can't.'

'Interesting,' said Homer. 'That's a good reason for her drowning.'

'Then what do you figure, Bull?'

'I figure this. She may have been pushed overboard!'

The sheriff gawked and pulled at his mustache. 'Well, I'll be damned!'

'Who's next, Shtunk?'

'Next I look for this Deming doll. I find

two snaps of her pan in the files. She is a model. I see her in a white bathing suit. I also see her in an evening gown. Not bad, that dame.'

'No news clippings?'

'No. These is just pictures, like snaps, on shiny paper.'

'Good enough.'

There was a pause. The Shtunk dug into his jacket and handed Homer a small picture.

'Here, Mr. Bull. The one in the evening dress.' Swink joined us in the belly laugh that followed.

'Gurney'll have your head,' said Homer. 'He's sure to miss that picture someday.'

'No, he ain't — I got the other one, too.'

'Why, Mr. Smith.' I wagged a finger at him. 'That's stealing!'

'Nuts, you lug — you're just jealous. Just for that I ain't showin' you the one in the bathing suit!'

Homer examined the back of the photograph. 'Olympe has told us a few truths, at any rate. This photograph has the stamp of the John Powers Model

Agency on its back.'

I toyed with the picture after Homer had finished with it. Olympe certainly had a classy chassis, and the picture was planned to merchandise it.

The Shtunk continued: 'I next go after Grace Lawrence. I find nothing you don't know about the dame, Mr. Bull.'

'Are you sure?' Homer eyed the Shtunk seriously. 'Her recent activities may prove interesting, and I haven't followed them. Any late clippings on Miss Lawrence?'

'Nothin'. Not since your divorce.'

'Go on.'

'I find some junk on Cunningham. But it is mostly from the business page of the *Times*. It is advertising stuff. He gets new business, so they give him space.'

'Any mention of Trum in the line of new business?'

'I don't see none. So I try for this Stanley Nevin.' The Shtunk shrugged. 'This guy Nevin is a blank. He don't rate even a line.'

'I didn't think he would. Did you try for him any other way? The phone book?'

'That was later. After I leave the clip

file, I decide to work on Gavano.'

Homer interrupted again. 'Hold on! You mean there wasn't anything on Gavano in that file?'

'Too much, Mr. Bull. But it is all junk. It is stuff on the big pinch in Brooklyn that time when the D. A. got hot all of a sudden on Mike's pinball racket. I know you don't want this corn, on account of it is stale stuff. I get a better idea. I decide to see an old pal. I look up my big shot chum from Red Hook — Pants Bader.'

'Who's Pants Bader?'

'I know Pants from old. We are kids together in Bensonhurst. Pants is a smart guy — he is a fancy stool, sort of, doing terrific business in Brooklyn. He's got two brothers in the bail bond line and he operates with uptown lawyers. I know Pants can dish plenty of dirt on Gavano on account of he is plenty mad at Mike, since Mike rubbed out a relative one time in a beer brawl on Rogers Avenue. That is why I go right to Bader.'

He finished his drink and backhanded his lips dry.

'Bader is hard to reach — but I find

him. He is glad to see me. It is easy to make him talk — all I got to do is mention Gavano, offhand. That starts him pitchin'. He tells me plenty of stuff, but it takes time and it's all mixed up.'

'Unmix it slowly,' said Homer.

'It ain't easy, Mr. Bull. Right off the bat I tell Pants like this: I say I hear Gavano is mixing with the big dough. Society. I mention Shipley. Nothing happens excepting Pants calls Gavano a few dirty names. But he gives me no angle. Then I ask Pants what Mike is doing these days in Brooklyn. Pants nearly busts a gut. He says something like: 'Since that big ape hooked up with Tina Pindo, he went yellow.''

He watched Homer scribble, in puzzled silence.

'That mean anything, Mr. Bull?'

'It's a lead. What else about Tina?'

I said: 'I remember a news story about Tina Pindo. She's Pindo's daughter. There was a small yam about her in the papers, after the pinball racket expose. Something about the innocent gal who didn't know her father was the biggest louse in Brooklyn. She ran away from

185

home when she found out. They got her later, about to leave the country. Old Pindo disappeared from the rackets after that. Father and daughter stuff.'

'That is correct, Mr. Bull. That is almost exactly like what Pants tells me. But Pants tells me more, later. He tells me he thinks Mike and Tina have got hooked. He has got the cockeyed idea that Gavano is going straight on account of a skirt.'

'Did you check his story?'

'Right away. I go to a phone booth and look for Gavano. I find a Gavano address, but it is out of town. This Gavano lives in a joint called Malverne, which is a small town dump on Long Island. I hop a train and go out there. Then I got to take a taxi to find the place — on account of it is a long walk, they tell me at the station. Sure enough, I catch the dame at home.'

'Mrs. Gavano?'

'Correct. She is a nice little mouse, I find. I ask her where is her husband Mike. She gives a little heave like she is scared of me. She tells me I have got the wrong Gavano, on account of her husband's name is Thomas. I see she is covering for Mike, but I can't get nowhere fast with her on account of she is still scared. So I act nice, tip my hat and leave.'

Homer was about to say something, but the Shtunk held up his hand.

'Maybe first I better finish with Gavano, Mr. Bull. I find out why it is absolutely a fact that Mike is living in this dump.'

'How?'

'I ask the cab driver if he knows the gink who lives in this house. He tells me he has seen him sometimes but does not know him. The cabby says he is a guy with a flock of gold in his mouth.'

'Wonderful!' said Homer. 'That's Mike, all right!'

'This is all I can get you on Mike, but I figure it is plenty on account of it is a different angle. I am right?'

Homer nodded. 'Now about Nevin?'

The Shtunk sighed. 'Yes and no, on Nevin. I check Nevin in the phone book and I find he is living in Westchester — in Scarsdale.'

I whistled. 'That's class.'

'No New York address?'

'Yeah. I find him on Fifth Avenue and Fifty-Seventh Street. It is a floozy dump, this building. I take the elevator to the tenth floor. It is room 1011. On the window I see: 'Stanley Nevin — Rare Books.' But the dump is locked, so I leave. I ask the kid in the elevator when I can see this Nevin guy. The kid tells me he ain't in town often — maybe two, three times a week. I try to pump the kid, but he don't know nothing. Then I call the Westchester place, but I get no answer.' He shrugged. 'I give up on Nevin. I grab a train and beat it up here.'

Swink ordered the next round, while we nibbled peanuts and potato chips and complimented the Shtunk.

He enjoyed the verbal backslaps, leaned forward on his elbows and grinned at Homer. 'I done good, Mr. Bull?'

'You've only started, Shtunk.'

'Only started? Where do I go next?'

'Back to town — on the next train. You'll be busy all night, or I miss my guess.'

14

Bedlam in the Bedrooms

Back in the car, Homer mooned over the pages of his little notebook while I toyed impatiently with the ignition key.

'What next?' I asked. 'I feel like a moron on a radio quiz program. This heckty-peckty is as clear as the Republican platform.'

'A bad analogy,' said Homer. 'The Republicans have only one platform. This case has two. Number one is the Shipley suicide, if it *was* a suicide. And number two is the Shipley book and all the cross-currents that lie behind it.'

'Fine and dandy, Homer. I apologize to the Republicans.'

'Forgetting the suicide for a moment,' he went on, 'the threads woven around the book point up a blind alley. Almost all of the guests want the book — before publication. The yacht affair would include

189

Trum, Nicky English and Cunningham. I'm not sure about Gavano. I can't quite place him in the mess. Nor can I explain Nevin, Olympe or Lester Minton. Who stole the notes from Eileen's house? Why? There's a connecting tissue between the book and the suicide, if I could only find the one small thread.'

I started the car and swung around toward Woodstock. 'Whither away, Homer?'

'Doctor Torrance's place.'

'You thinking of breaking in? Wouldn't a big house like that have a caretaker?'

'I doubt it. Swink would have taken me through if there was a caretaker.'

Homer was right, as usual. I parked behind a big barn abutting on the road. Homer got out.

'Take a short ride for yourself, Hank.'

'Why can't I come along? I'm an expert at opening windows.'

'Bad technique. I don't want anybody to notice the car, sonny. Pick me up in about fifteen minutes.'

I drove back to Kingston slowly, juggling the jigsaw pieces the Shtunk had added to the puzzle. What puzzle? Where was the murder mystery? *Had* Shipley been murdered? How? Where was the murderer? Homer must have found something, or we would have left Woodstock on the afternoon train. I retraced the pattern of events, groping for an answer to Homer's unflagging interest in the mess.

Why had Shipley invited Homer? They were only casual acquaintances. Did Shipley know that his cast of characters at the party would interest him? Or did the invitation have a deeper significance — a promise of mayhem? Then of course, there was Grace Lawrence. Perhaps Shipley thought that he would enjoy the byplay between Trum and Homer?

Gavano suggested an answer to something, somehow. Was he really Shipley's bodyguard? That would mean that Hugo Shipley was afraid of somebody. It was a silly idea, until I suddenly thought of Lester. Lester had worked for Pindo. Mike had married Pindo's daughter. At that point, the unforged link snapped under the feeble fire of my deduction.

I scratched my nose and forgot about

Gavano. How about Trum? Was there any connection between Cunningham and Trum, other than business? Could be. The idea of a cigarette tycoon making a weekend trip to talk about artwork didn't ring true. Big businessmen leave such petty details to their advertising lackeys. Oh sure, they'll okay a special art job once in a while. But not very often. It was phoney. The idea of Trum begging Shipley to do the naked dames for his cigarette ads was phoney, I deduced. Trum either came up for an innocuous weekend in the country, or he had another, stronger reason for the trip to Shipley's.

Olympe played havoc with my imagination. A doll with a frame as stimulating as hers might very well have posed for Shipley's succulent heroines. Why, then, the gag about a secretary? Was it Shipley's idea? Olympe may have played hard to get in New York. Shipley was a notorious heel with the softer sex. Maybe he figured she'd be easier to handle, once under his roof? I crossed this idea out fast. Olympe was no innocent bunny. Olympe could smell that gag in a minute. So what?

Could it be that she was in love with Shipley? Could be.

Back at the barn, Homer was waiting for me. I looked at my watch. I had been gone only twelve minutes. He couldn't have been inside already.

'Give up?' I asked.

'It was easy. The good doctor forgot to board up a cellar window. I kicked it in.'

'Get what you wanted?'

'All of it. I wanted the doctor's record on Shipley. I found his file in order, and got the complete medical outline on Hugo from 1936 until last Thursday.'

'Good gravy!' I yapped. 'Was Shipley that sick?'

'I don't know. Haven't read it yet. But the fact that Hugo went to the doctor since 1936 may not mean that he was sick at all. Some people use doctors regularly — for periodic check-ups.'

There was a five-mile silence.

I sighed wearily. 'A helluva comic strip case this is going to make — even if Shipley was murdered. It'll take you months to rewrite this thing for your readers.'

'Nonsense. I can write this thing in less

than a week, Hank. All I need is a murder.'

I skidded around the last turn and through the gate to the house. Lester rid us of our coats in the main hall.

'You gents want coffee? They're all in the dinin' room.'

Homer nodded him away.

I said: 'Isn't it funny — this sudden change in the bedtime hours? Last night every one of these people was in the arms of Morpheus at this hour. Tonight — '

He chuckled.

'Don't you allow for the effect of a suicide and two sluggings on these people?'

'They didn't seem excited a while ago.'

The coffee *klatch* was gathered in the long dining hall, for dining room it had never been. It was extra-long, extra-high, extra-massive — a hodgepodge of hooked-up trappings and casement windows. A heavy oak table stretched the full length of the room.

Olympe Deming poured. 'We've missed you, Mr. Bull.'

'Thank you.' Homer smiled around the table. 'You miss me, too, Mike?'

'Oh, yeah. I'm worryin' myself stiff about you boys. Where you been?'

'We went down to the drugstore for some aspirin,' I said. 'You need any aspirin, Mike?'

'I got no headache.'

'You can never tell about headaches,' said Homer with a smile. 'You might get one at any moment, you know.'

Grace asked: 'How's your head, Homer?'

'So-so.' He blushed.

'Stop by at my room later, honey,' she cooed. 'I've got the swellest tablets for that sort of thing. Much, much better than silly old aspirin.'

'You're very kind, Grace.'

I watched Trum redden to the gills. Homer played with his spoon, exchanging chit-chat with Olympe. There was an unpleasant spot of silence around the table. I counted the heads. Cunningham sat opposite, turning his long jaw to Grace Lawrence occasionally. Trum sat at her side, sucking his lip. There were heavy bags under his eyes, and his fat face was paler than usual. I couldn't find Stanley Nevin.

'Nevin gone to bed?' I asked Nicky.

Nicky looked up from his glass of Scotch sleepily. 'Went upstairs for his pipe.'

At that moment there was a shout from upstairs.

'I say — down there — come and see what's happened to my room. Somebody's ransacked it!' It was Nevin's voice.

Everybody got up at once, in a pell-mell dash for the stairs. Homer and I held the lead and were the first to barge into Nevin's room. He stood in the doorway, his handsome face full of real alarm. Homer closed the door on the others.

The room was a mess. Every drawer in the chest was out, and Nevin's wardrobe was scattered on the floor, on the bed and piled in funny disarray on the easy chair in the corner. The bed itself had been unmade, upheaved and turned inside out — a confusion of sheets, blankets and a mattress. Two suitcases lay asprawl this heap, emptied on the bedding. It was a nightmare of sudden search. And sudden seizure?

'Anything missing?' Homer asked.

'I — I don't know yet. But I can't understand what anybody would want — '

'Money? Jewelry?'

'My money's in my wallet. I haven't any jewelry worth stealing.'

He searched the pile of stuff on the beds. 'There doesn't seem to be anything missing.'

'Have you been downstairs all evening, Nevin?'

He nodded. 'In the library, mostly.'

'Then this could have happened any time tonight?'

'Any time from about seven to midnight.'

Homer sat on the bed. 'Tell me, Nevin — aside from money and jewelry, would there be anything else you own that might interest a thief?'

Nevin was puzzled. 'What do you mean? What else could I have?'

'The notes. Shipley's book notes.'

I saw sudden anger in Nevin's eyes. But he let it die.

'I didn't get them and they weren't taken from my room,' Nevin snapped.

Someone knocked, and I opened the door. It was Nicky English. His face was greenish-white. He looked sick with rage.

'What the hell goes on, Bull?' he almost screamed. 'If you think this room is bad, you ought to see what some louse has done to mine!'

Nicky's room was at the head of the stairs. We found it in the same state of disorder. Whoever the searcher was, he had done a more thorough job here. Even the rug was turned back in one corner. Nicky was brief and to the point.

'No harm done,' he said. 'Nothing missing. Somebody played a bum hunch. I've got nothing worth stealing anyhow.'

Homer paused in the door. 'See here, English. I believe you've got something — some angle on this business — that may be important. I'm willing to share the glory. I don't want the news story — you can break it in your column. I'd just like to know why in hell you're playing hard to get.'

'Still beating around the bush, eh, Bull? Didn't you get any dope from New York?'

'Plenty. But I can't make it fit. I can't

see, for example, how Marie Parrish fits into this case.'

Nicky leered in his face. 'Trying for a rise out of me, eh? Let me give you a tip, Bull. Keep your nose out of that mess — that's mine!'

'Then you know who pushed Marie into the sea?'

Nicky laughed us into the hall and lit a cigarette. 'You're not so dumb, Bull. Maybe tomorrow — '

Lester came running upstairs, followed by Minnie and the others. 'I just been back to my room, Mr. Bull. Somebody been through it with a fine-toothed comb!'

'It's robbery, that's what it is,' Minnie shrilled. 'I say we should call the police!'

They made a funny pair, those two. I couldn't restrain the cackle that rose in my throat and became a number-one belly laugh before I could swallow it. Cunningham joined me in the laugh, and I thought I heard Grace Lawrence's husky gurgle add to the merriment.

Nicky didn't think it funny. 'You crumb cartoonists are all alike!' he shot at me.

'You seem to have a corner on idiotic humor!'

I didn't like that. I stepped forward to shove his sharp face into the wall behind him. But Homer caught my arm. He stepped between us nimbly.

'Go ahead, MacAndrew, I've been waiting for this for years,' Cunningham laughed. 'Nicky won't hit back. He only strikes back through his column.'

Nicky was flustered, even his tongue. He turned on Cunningham. 'Why, you cheap advertising pimp!' He began. 'I oughta — '

But he never finished. Cunningham eased his big frame within striking distance and let fly. A sharp right cross smacked Nicky's head back. It was a clean hit. Nicky caved in all at once, and before anyone could catch him he was rolling head over tail down the stairway in front of us.

There was a short squeal from Grace. 'My God! You've killed him!'

'Not a chance,' said Cunningham. 'Rats don't die that easily!' He turned on his heel and walked away toward his room.

Downstairs, Nicky lay in an angular heap, his head thrown back against the wall and lumped and bloody from caressing the stairs.

Nevin leaned over him. 'He's hurt badly. Better carry him up to his room, Lester.'

Lester touched Nicky gingerly, and his eyes flickered open. He shrugged Lester away.

'Leggo!' he snarled, and rose slowly.

But he didn't stand long. After a few steps, his knees sagged and he hit the floor again. Lester lifted him easily and carried him upstairs.

'Better call that doctor again,' said Homer.

We followed Lester to the phone.

'Stay with English for a while, Hank.'

'What for? If he comes to, he won't care for my bedside manner!'

'You mustn't let me forget to look in on Nicky later, Hank.'

'He's all right, Homer. He'll live.'

'Will he? I hope so. I have a question to ask Nicky English — a very, very important question.'

15

Grace Gives Out

Minnie Minton fluttered around the room, setting it straight. She finished making her bed, gave it a final slap and sat down with a sigh.

'Now — ?' she said, eyeing Homer brightly.

'Now, Minnie,' he began, 'who do you suppose upset your room tonight?'

'I wish I knew, sir. I just wish I knew! It's a cryin' shame, that's what it is — all these goings on, I mean. Who, you ask? I say, how should I know? Fifteen years it is I've been in this line, sir — and never once — well, yes, there was one time when something like this — '

'You were in the kitchen preparing for tomorrow at about the time when Mr. MacAndrew and I were hit in the studio, isn't that right?'

'Yes, sir.'

'You went to your room after that?'

'Why no, sir. Fact is, I went out — went for a walk over to Eileen's. I always walk a bit, after hours. Does me good, sir. Lots of times Lester, he comes with me and we just idle around for a few hours outdoors. Not that he — well, yes, I guess it was around eight when I got there.'

'And you returned?'

She eyed the ceiling for the exact time. 'Must have been around eleven, sir, or a little after.'

'But you didn't go to your room then?'

'No, indeed,' she piped. 'Oh, no, indeed. I — well, fact is, I was thirsty, sir. Eileen, the dear woman, she treated me to a new dish — anchovy paste on toast, it was, with cream cheese. And a treat it is, at that. But I did have the thirst afterwards — an awful thirst for a cup of coffee, as you can understand.'

'It's one of my favorites,' said Homer, 'especially with a portion of eggs flavored with wine on the toast. You found Lester here when you returned?'

She shook her head. 'He came in after a bit.'

'You mean he'd been outdoors?'

'I suppose, but I don't know, that he was probably out with that Eyetalian again, though I shouldn't say for sure he was, at that.'

'You mean Gavano.'

'I do.' She nodded queerly. 'A man should always pick his own friends, I always say, and I'm not the wife to be interfering. Though I do think that man is full of evil. But then, Lester and him — well, they're old friends by now, and I may be all wrong, for no harm's come of it.'

'Lester knew him before this job?'

'Oh, no, sir! I wouldn't say that at all. This Eyetalian has been up here, off and on, a good few years now. Not regular, mind you — but he has some duties to do for Mr. Shipley from time to time. Though he wasn't a servant ever, if you ask me, what with him sleeping upstairs with the rest. Never on weekends, sir, mind you. This is the first time. Mostly he came during the week, and didn't stay for long.'

Lester came in and stood near the bed

until Minnie screamed him into a chair.

'Have you any idea, Lester, who might have upset the three bedrooms tonight?'

He shook his head dumbly.

'You weren't in your room, from early evening until just a while ago?'

'No.'

'Where were you?'

'Outside, mostly. I went out for a walk.'

Minnie half turned in her seat to snap: 'With that Eyetalian, I suppose?'

His pig eyes opened wide. 'Who says so?'

'I says so!' she mocked.

'Were you with Gavano, Lester?'

He set his lips stubbornly. 'No!'

'Where did you walk?'

'Down the road. Toward Woodstock.'

'Why did you go to Woodstock?'

'Probably for beer,' chirped Minnie. 'Catch him walking that far for anything else!'

'Did you go for a beer?' Homer asked.

'I went for a walk, I tell ya.'

'What time did you get back?'

'Around eleven.'

'Did you enter any store in town?'

'I didn't get to Woodstock,' he muttered. 'Got far as that Apple Rock; then I came back.'

It was possible. The Apple Rock sat on the edge of town, about a quarter of a mile away from the shops. A fast walker could make it in under two hours.

'What did you do after you returned?'

'Cleaned up ashtrays in the living room. When I come back to the kitchen, I see Minnie and we have coffee.'

'Can you remember who was in the living room when you got there?'

'Everybody. No — Mr. Nevin was reading in the library.'

'You sure, now, that Gavano was with them?' Homer asked sharply. 'Remember, it's an easy matter for me to ask inside about Gavano. He isn't the sort of person they'd forget seeing, Lester.'

There was a long pause while Lester remembered. 'I ain't sure.'

Minnie snorted. 'He ain't sure. Foosh!'

Homer thanked them, and we left.

Downstairs, the big clock bonged once in the quiet of the hall. The sound died slowly in the shadows, the death knell of

Tuesday's first hour. Somewhere over the hills, a hoarse dog yelped into the night. I shivered and followed Homer up the stairs.

At Grace's door, he knocked gently.

Grace managed a cheery grin and made us comfortable. She had on a silk lounging gown that fell in a broad flare from her well-rounded hips, where the red bodice played hob with her torso. Grace was getting on. Her brittle manikin's figure had given in to the way of all flesh. This was no longer a figure to be snapped in tight-fitting clothes, or the statuesque poses of *Vanity Fair*. But it looked well in a bedroom. Very.

She lit a cigarette and faced Homer nervously. 'Like old times, isn't it, honey?'

'Almost.' Homer smiled.

She inhaled a long drag. 'I know what you're thinking, Homer. You've got it all figured, about me and Trum.'

'Have I?'

'But you're wrong. It's not what you think.'

She looked at him hopefully. There was a long silence, then:

207

'Is that what you wanted to tell me, Grace?'

I got up and said: 'Maybe I'd better scram, and leave you two love birds to twitter alone.'

'Better stay,' said Homer. 'If old man Trum should ever find me in here alone, the fat'll fly!'

Grace was hurt. 'Please stay, Hank. And don't be so funny, Homer. Trum won't come in here at this hour. Trum is — oh hell, will you listen to me? Will you?'

Homer caught the sob in her voice and apologized.

'I came up here for a reason, Homer, but Trum was only — well, it was because of those Shipley drawings that I came here.'

'I heard about them.'

'I met Trum through Cunningham,' she went on. 'I'd known Cunningham through the agency work I used to do. He cooked up the idea of a series of pictures to rival the Petty women — you know, the Old Gold ads. Cunningham introduced me to Trum at a party. Naturally I was anxious to tie up with the idea — it would have made swell publicity for me. I met Cunningham last week. He told me that he didn't think Shipley would go for the idea. He received an invitation for this weekend party soon after I saw him. Then Trum called me and suggested that I come up here with them.'

'That sounds perfectly all right to me,' said Homer. 'Perfectly straight.'

'It *is* straight,' she almost pleaded. 'I don't want you to think that Trum — good Lord, Homer, I haven't sunk that low. The old boy is sweet on me, I'll admit. I didn't mind him — he was harmless. Matter of fact, he's the original schoolboy type — he's proposed marriage to me already.'

'A good catch.'

'Good?' I said. 'Five or six dames have already thrown him back!'

Grace wasn't done.

'Let me finish, Hank. I drove up here alone, and Shipley was very nice to me. But — I don't know — from the very first night I felt funny about things — about the whole party, I mean. Shipley told me that he'd asked you up here. I tried to find out why, but he wouldn't tell me. He seemed to have something up his sleeve, some joke I couldn't quite understand.'

Homer came alive. 'What do you mean, Grace?'

'I wish I could put it in words. It reminded me of a surprise party. You know how they do — everybody hides until the victim arrives, and then they all jump out from behind the furniture and yell: 'Surprise.' That was sort of the feeling I had, except that I felt all along that Shipley would be the man to jump out and yell. It was his choice of guests that got me, I guess.'

'I've heard that before, from Swink. Did anything happen to bear out your suspicions?'

'Nothing — and everything. Why should a group of people make me feel afraid? Yes, I was afraid. I liked hardly any of them. I couldn't stand Nicky English. He seemed hell bent on raising trouble — always teasing Shipley and Trum, and even Cunningham.'

'Teasing?'

She struggled for the right word. 'Oh!
— not teasing, exactly. There seemed to
be an undercurrent of spite and hate and
bad feeling between all these people. It
was the sort of thing you could sense,
somehow.'

'Did you feel it with Olympe?'

She nodded. 'All of them, I said. Even
Nevin, the college boy. He's too quiet. He
sat in a corner, well out of all the
conversation, never saying a word, just
watching. And then, of course, that awful
pug, Gavano!' She snubbed her cigarette.
'I was actually going to leave on Sunday
afternoon — it got me that bad.'

'Why didn't you go?'

'I'm sorry I stayed. Trum insisted that
he'd talk it out with Shipley that evening.
I was anxious to find out whether I'd get
the job. It meant a lot to me.'

'But all this time, nothing happened?'

'I'm getting to that,' she said. 'Shipley
started it. I'd heard stories about his
queer parties, so I wasn't really surprised
to see Gavano among us. Shipley
introduced him as his best friend. I
thought it was a gag at first. I remember

that Cunningham did laugh at the introduction. But Shipley was serious. Gavano ate with us. Shipley had him at his side up until — '

'The suicide?'

'Yes. Until that night.'

'Can you remember what Shipley actually said about Gavano?'

'Actually, he said nothing. Nothing but the fact that Gavano was his friend. He said that often. He made a point of repeating it. Smugly.'

'Perhaps he meant it.'

Grace laughed softly. 'You don't know Shipley. He meant something else, I'm sure. You knew it by the way he smirked when he said it. There was something evil about it all, I tell you. But that isn't the worst. It was after Shipley had — on the day after, it seemed to me, things began to happen.'

'I think I know what follows,' said Homer. 'You're coming to the business about the book, aren't you?'

She nodded.

'Let's go back a bit,' said Homer. 'You knew about the book all along, of course?'

'I couldn't help but know. Trum talked about it whenever we met Eileen. He made a point of asking her cute little questions about the damn book. And he'd sometimes talk about it with me. It seemed to bother him.'

'Did he tell you why?'

'No. It was all very casual. But this morning — '

'Monday morning?'

'Yes — it was after breakfast that I noticed for the first time that Trum had changed. As a matter of fact, the whole guest list seemed happier after Shipley died. It's a cruel thing to say, but it's true.'

'You'll have to explain that one, Grace.'

'I'll try. The first thing I noticed was that Gavano suddenly became a part of the group. Cunningham, Trum and English no longer shied away from him. It seemed odd to me. But I thought it might be the result of the suicide — you know how people get after a death.'

Homer had finally taken out his book. 'You mean that Trum, Cunningham and English hadn't spoken to Gavano at all before Monday morning?'

'Only a word, at most. But it was different on Monday. I saw each one of them talking to Gavano at different times. Once I saw Nicky English on the terrace. I didn't hear what was said. But they were talking earnestly — at least Nicky was. Another time it was Cunningham. And finally — '

'Trum, of course.'

She got up and moved close to Homer. 'That's why I wanted to see you tonight. I might have saved you that beating in the studio. If I'd had any brains, I'd have spoken to you sooner. But I didn't realize — you see, it began after you spoke to all of us in the living room yesterday afternoon. When the little party broke up, Trum and I walked out on the porch for a while. He kept looking over toward the Tucker place. He said: 'I wonder if Bull will have her retype those stolen notes.' He said it casually, as though he were playing at being a detective. Then he said: 'I'd give a lot to know what Shipley was writing about.''

'That was all?'

'Not exactly. I — well, I teased him a bit about his past. He froze up completely after that. Then I promptly forgot about our little conversation. But later on, I was reminded of it again. I should have warned you. It was after dinner. I'd gone to my room. I came out after a while and started down the hall. Just as I left my door, I saw a man going into Trum's room. It was Gavano!'

'He didn't see you?'

'He was almost through the door, and he didn't turn my way. I should have known then what might happen. But it never occurred to me that Trum would use Gavano to get those notes from you, Homer. If I'd thought quickly, perhaps all this might easily have been avoided.'

Homer rose and patted her cheek. 'I always said you had a heart of gold beneath that frosted face, Grace. It's nice to know that you still worry about me.'

She smiled a sad smile. 'Why don't you quit this business up here, Homer? I'm afraid, really I am.'

'Not much further to worry,' he chuckled. 'I have a feeling we'll be leaving here tomorrow night.'

'Before the inquest?' I asked. 'I thought you were having an inquest on Wednesday.'

'Maybe I've changed my mind, Hank.'

She stood in the doorway touching Homer's arm, and the bedroom eyes were burning high voltage.

'Good night, Grace. Tomorrow's a big day.'

When he turned, halfway down the hall, she was still in the doorway. I caught the gesture of a slowly blown kiss.

Homer shrugged at the rag.

'Dames is peculiar,' he said.

16

A Crumb from Trum

Homer pecked away at his noiseless portable. I dragged slowly on my cigarette, waiting for him to knock off and let me sleep.

'More notes?' I asked. 'Notes seem to be the vogue up here. You think it was Gavano who conked us?'

'Can't be sure.' He flipped the sheet out of the machine and laid it away in his bag. 'But whoever it was must be mighty worried, Hank. More than that — he's afraid.'

'Afraid of what?'

'The answer to that one will have to wait. This business of the notes has kept me up here, sonny. Why should anybody lay into us for Eileen's transcribed version of the first chapter? It's silly, because anybody knows that Eileen can do the same job for us again.'

'I never thought of it that way.'

'It's the key, it seems to me. Let's assume that our mysterious mauler was the man or woman who stole the whole mess of stuff from Eileen's house. This person knew that Eileen was retyping as much as she had done on the book originally. He wants to find out one important thing, Hank — did Eileen read all the notes, *including the part that Shipley had handwritten*? Was she going to give us a complete record of all these notes? Or would it be only the first chapter? Don't forget — our thief has the first chapter in his possession. He knows that it's meaningless material. He then begins to worry. Maybe he worries this way: If Eileen has read the rest of the notes, he'd like to know about it! He'd like to know *just how much* of the handwritten stuff Eileen has remembered.'

'You mean that the real poison was written by Shipley in longhand?'

'Exactly. The fact that we were slugged in the studio proves this point. But can you think of any other reason for our man slugging us? There's another one.'

I shook my head. 'Keep it.'

'Not so fast, Hank — you're not thinking it through. There's another angle — the angle that's been gnawing at me ever since I spoke to Eileen. It's this: Let's assume that the entire batch of notes was stolen from the Tuckers by Trum. That leaves English, Cunningham, Nevin and Olympe still in the running. Of these four, suppose only English and Cunningham have a strong reason, I mean a reason as strong as Trum's, for wanting to see that first chapter. Trum has the notes, remember. Thus, either Cunningham or English might be tempted to conk us for a glimpse at that first chapter. Do you follow me?'

'Vaguely. But isn't that silly? I mean — doesn't it seem more logical the first way?'

'It's the obvious conclusion, yes. I'd like to let it go on that. But — '

There was a soft knock at the door.

'Omigod!' I snorted. 'MacAndrew doesn't sleep after all. Who the hell is that?'

'That would be Mr. Trum.'

And it was. The roly-poly cigarette mogul stood in the doorway, wrapped in a black and grey bathrobe that couldn't quite hide his magenta-striped pajamas.

'You'll excuse me, Bull,' he said falteringly. 'But I couldn't sleep until I saw you. I've been waiting up for you, you know.'

Trum sat on the edge of his chair, playing with his hands. He pulled out a handkerchief and blew his nose. He fumbled with a big black cigarette case and tremblingly lit a long one.

'I hardly know how to tell you what's on my mind, Bull. I feel — well, damn it! — I feel actually frightened!'

Homer sat up. 'What do you mean by that? Anybody threaten you?'

Trum shifted his rear. 'Well, not exactly. And yet it was a threat. It's made me afraid.' He mopped his brow. 'Perhaps I'd better start from the beginning.'

'Good!' said Homer. 'You'll tell me why you came up this weekend first, of course?'

That was a body blow. Trum wasn't

prepared for it. He shrugged finally. 'Why not? It was the book.'

'Not the advertising drawings, then?'

He shook his head. 'I don't have to take weekend trips to get artwork, Bull. But I'd heard stories from Cunningham about Shipley's scandalous book. I say scandalous because Cunningham told me so. The book was to be filled with all sorts of ugly stories about people — about Shipley's friends. I came up here to buy Hugo off, frankly. I had a good reason for stopping his reminiscences.'

'Marie Parrish?'

He nodded grimly. 'It was a most unfortunate affair. Bull, believe me, I've done some pretty stupid things in my day — especially with the ladies. But this was an accident. You see, I'd been drinking that night, heavily. Marie was a very attractive woman. We were — well, we were both pretty tight, I guess. I — oh, you understand what happens in such cases. I thought she wouldn't resent me. She — well, she fell overboard.'

'You didn't push her?'

'Good heavens, no!'

'Why didn't you call for help?'

'I would have if I'd been sober. But I passed out. Passed out cold, I tell you. When I came to, Shipley and Cunningham told me what had happened. I wanted to avoid a scandal. People would certainly assume that I — well, they'd assume what you have, Bull. I decided to keep quiet about the whole affair. It was Cunningham's idea. It worked pretty well, you'll remember. The doctors found alcohol in her stomach, and the affair was written off as an accident. There was only one person who gave me any trouble about the thing — '

'Nicky English?'

'How did you know? Yes, it was English. Of course, he had no evidence. But that didn't prevent him from publishing innuendoes in his column, nor from continually bothering me, thinking — '

'Blackmail, eh?'

'No, Nicky didn't want any money. But it wasn't long before members of my crew began to come to me with stories about Nicky. He had been around the boat, offering money for information. He tried each of the men in turn, but, of course, he got nothing out of them — they hadn't seen the thing happen. Then he came to my office one day and tried to frighten me into telling him the truth about the thing.'

'During all this, was there any possibility of Nicky knowing what had happened on the boat?'

'Not by a long shot. Cunningham and Shipley were the only men who actually knew, and neither of them would tell Nicky. They both had a strong dislike for the man, as you know.'

'You were never threatened by either Shipley or Cunningham?'

He shook his head. 'They were my friends.'

'Cunningham's agency handles your cigarette advertising. Did he have the account before the Parrish affair?'

'Well — no. You see, I was grateful to Cunningham. I gave him the account, however, of my own free will, you understand. I've never had reason to be sorry — he's a good advertising man.'

'What happened when Nicky came to your office?'

'I threw him out!'

'This is the first time you've seen him since then?'

'Yes. Naturally, when I met Nicky up here, I became more alarmed than ever about Shipley's book, though I couldn't imagine why Hugo had asked the man up here. I decided, just after Hugo died, that I'd better get those story notes as quickly as possible. You can understand, now, why I had to have them.'

'Naturally. You wanted to make sure that Shipley hadn't told about the Marie Parrish affair.'

Trum mopped his head and sighed. 'I was desperate. I knew that Nicky English would stop at nothing to lay his hands on that manuscript. At first I thought of trying to buy the whole business from Eileen. But I was afraid. I knew she wasn't the type — that she wouldn't take dirty money. It occurred to me to use Mike Gavano. I made an appointment with him. It was a stupid thing to do. I've regretted it.'

'You told Gavano what you wanted?'

'Only that I wanted the notes — I didn't tell him why. He said that it'd be easy.'

'How much did you offer him?'

'Five thousand.'

'Wow!' I yipped. 'That must have set Mr. Gavano's fertile brain a-whizzing.'

'It was a mistake,' said Homer. 'Even if Gavano had stolen the notes, you wouldn't have bought them at that price, Trum.'

'I realized that too late. At any rate, after your questioning Eileen in the living room yesterday afternoon, I gave up all hope. Somebody else had stolen the notes. I saw Gavano later in the day — after dinner, to be exact. I told him to forget about our little deal. I got the shock of my life, Bull — Gavano told me that he already had the notes!'

'Did he show them to you?'

'No. He only said they were 'plenty hot,' and that they were worth much more than five thousand dollars.'

Homer whistled. 'I think Gavano was bluffing, Trum. He probably felt that he had a chance to get the notes from the original thief. And, too, it gave him something in his own line to mess around with until Wednesday.'

Trum lit another cigarette. 'I'm pretty sure he was bluffing, Bull. I think I know who has those notes.'

'Nicky English?'

Trum almost dropped his cigarette. 'How in the world did you know that?'

'I didn't. I'm stabbing. But how do *you* know?'

'I was alone in the library for quite a while this evening — Shipley has an admirable collection of Hogarth, a favorite of mine. I spent about an hour going through his plates and then wandered out on the terrace. I saw you and MacAndrew return from the Tuckers'. I won't deny that I was curious to know whether you had any part of that first chapter. I knew you'd have her try to redo it from memory.'

'You have a detective's mind, Trum.'

'At any rate, I left the terrace for my room. After a while, I came downstairs again, and stood in the dining room for a moment, I don't know why. As you know, it's possible to see the studio door from almost any part of the dining room. The hall to the studio was lit. I say that because my eyesight is none too good. If that light hadn't been lit, I couldn't have seen the door, nor the man who ran out of it quite suddenly.'

'You recognized the man?'

'I couldn't be sure — he was running, you know. But I could almost swear it was Nicky English.'

Homer leaned back in his chair, his eyes half closed. 'You noticed the way he was dressed?'

'No.'

'In spite of the fact that you didn't see him well, you still identify him as Nicky English?'

'Only because of what happened later. I followed the man through the main hall — '

'Just a moment, Trum! Did you see the man running down the main hall?'

Trum shook his head.

'Then you aren't sure he ran down the main hall? He could have run through the dining room, onto the terrace, isn't that right?'

Trum squirmed. 'Of course it's right. I took for granted the fact that he would run down the hall. That was why I went directly toward the front of the house — toward the library.'

'I'm not saying that he didn't run down the main hall, Trum. I'm only suggesting that your man might have gone through other rooms — rooms you didn't search. You didn't examine the living room and the terrace, did you?'

'No, I didn't. I went directly to the library. When I got there, I saw Nicky English. He was coming out.'

'How was he dressed?'

Trum wrinkled his fat brows. 'That's odd, Bull; I can't say that I remember.'

'Nicky was wearing a tweed jacket and buff-colored slacks all day,' said Homer. 'Don't you think you would have recalled that ensemble if the man who ran out of the studio had worn it?'

Trum shrugged. 'I haven't much of an eye for clothes.'

'You must excuse my interruptions,

Trum. I'm not trying to clear Nicky English — not by a long shot. But if you want to identify him as my assailant, we'll have to have clearer proof.'

'I understand. I was getting to that. You see, when I met Nicky in the library, he seemed exceptionally sly and sharp with me. It seemed that he was playing cat to my canary, if you get what I mean. He asked me whether I'd yet seen any part of Shipley's book. I told him I hadn't. He insinuated that it'd make excellent material for his column. He seemed to be warning me — to be buying my silence — '

'You mean that he knew you had seen him from the dining room?'

'Oh, I can't be sure of that, Bull. I can't be sure. It was all innuendo, mind you — all innuendo.'

'But it might have been just Nicky's normal manner of speech.'

There was a confused silence. 'I suppose so.'

'You left the library with Nicky?'

'No, I remained there.'

'How long?'

'I couldn't say, Bull. But I got out of there when I saw the doctor come by the hall. I followed him into the studio.'

Homer arose to end the interview. 'You've been very helpful, Trum — in many ways. No need to worry any more about — those notes.'

Trum eyed him quizzically for a moment and said good night. Homer turned from the door and went rapidly to his table near the window.

'You think Trum was leveling, Homer?'

'Leveling?' He shot me a quick smile. 'Trum's afraid, Hank. He's scared stiff!'

'Scared? I thought he looked relieved after he spilled his yarn. Seemed glad to get it off his chest.'

'Maybe. Trum's a clever man, sonny. I think he came in here tonight to set himself straight with me. I think he's afraid — afraid that Gavano might have conked us in the studio.'

'Then you don't think it was Nicky?'

'We'll find out, Hank — right now!'

I eyed my watch. 'Right now? It's almost three. Nicky must be asleep; he's a sick boy.'

'I have an idea he's awake. Scandal columnists don't usually hit the hay before breakfast time, especially when they're working on a story. This is Nicky's creative hour.'

'In spite of the trouncing he got tonight?'

'You handed him his briefcase, didn't you?'

I nodded. 'You think that means he's still working?'

'Unless the drug put him to sleep. I have an idea that Nicky English would work all night to finish the story he had in mind, Hank. We've got to see him — and right away.'

It sounded logical. Homer had been guessing right for ten hours and running. But this was the eleventh hour. How was I to know that this hunch could be wrong?

Dead wrong!

17

Droopydrawers Gets His!

We minced down the hall to Nicky's room. Faint streaks of moonlight silvered the long window at the far end of the corridor. But the hall was dark and quiet. Too quiet. Somewhere outside, the wind played a dirge on a tree.

Homer rapped on the door gently, then rapped again. He put his ear to the door and listened. Then he stooped to squint through the keyhole.

'I'll be damned. Take a look, Hank.'

I looked. There wasn't a light in the room. The faint moonlight showed me Nicky's bed, empty. I don't know why I shivered. It may have been the weird light that gave the simple scene the quality of horror. Or perhaps, I thought, the sound of Homer's breathing, over my left shoulder, made me tremble.

Homer tried the knob, and his right

eyebrow went up. 'Locked!' he whispered. 'Get our door key, Hank. I discovered this afternoon that all these doors have the same lock.'

I returned with the key and he opened the door. Inside, he shut it softly behind us. When I made for the light switch, he banged my arm down sharply.

'No need for light, Hank. The moon is bright enough.'

'For what?'

'Look for the notes,' he whispered. 'And hop to it — I'd hate to have Nicky walk in on us.'

I opened the bathroom door and peered into the gloom until my eyes caught the dull specks of light on the bathtub hardware. Then the moon played hard to get behind a cloud. The hardware highlights faded. I stood in the middle of the room near the tub, waiting for the moon.

The light came suddenly, showing me a wall of shower curtains. I pulled them apart, and horror clutched at my guts. I felt my stomach turn over and my heart pound in my ears.

A grey shape hung from the metal rod above. It was Nicky English! His eyes bulged, fishlike, and stared me back into the bedroom. I almost fell into Homer's arms.

'Nicky!' I gasped, pointing a shaking finger into the john. 'Stiff!'

Then I slumped into a chair and felt my arteries harden. The light clicked on in the bathroom. Off again. Homer skipped around the bedroom.

'The key,' he muttered, and back he went to the john.

My stomach fell back in its groove. I joined Homer.

'Get a blanket, Hank. We'll cover the window in here. I need light.'

I hung a blanket over the small window, and he snapped on the light.

Nicky hung by a red cord, knotted at the far end of the heavy shower fixture. It was grisly. His arms hung limp; his long robe seemed ready to drop from his shoulders at a sneeze. The broad sleeves hid his hands completely.

I was studying the contrast of purple robe against his bandaged green face when Homer beckoned me to the sink. He stood over a small mound of ashes.

'Nicky burned his bridges behind him,' he said.

'Small bridges. Why should Nicky burn papers in the sink?'

'Why should Nicky commit suicide?' Homer countered, scraping the ashes into an envelope. 'Hold the fort — I'm going to call Swink!'

How easy it had been to hate Nicky! But why should he commit suicide? I plunged back over the trail of evidence for a reason. Could Nicky have killed Shipley? The charred note pointed to that sort of a mess. But how? And why would he kill Shipley, even if it were possible? Could it be that Shipley had been the man who took Marie Parrish aboard Trum's yacht? It was a motive. I remembered suddenly that we didn't yet know the answer to the Marie Parrish business. After all, Nicky might have discovered that Shipley had withheld information about the accident. Nicky was supposed to have been madly in love with Marie. He hadn't, since then, been tied up with any other heart interest. He might have been waiting for a chance to get even with Shipley.

Homer returned and scampered into the john. He came out holding aloft the missing key.

'It was in his pocket.'

'Meaning which?'

'Meaning, I suppose, that Nicky locked the door, put the key in his pocket, burned almost all of the Shipley book notes, and stepped off the stool into eternity.'

'Neat. But why?'

Homer disregarded my question. He had found Nicky's briefcase, hidden on a shelf in the closet. He pulled out a sheaf of papers and thumbed through them. They were standard letter size sheets of typewriting paper — all blank! In a side pocket Homer found a fountain pen, a few pencils and an eraser. He tried the pen. It was full.

'Queerer and queerer,' he said. 'You're quite sure you handed him his briefcase?'

I nodded. 'Positive.'

'It didn't — it couldn't have slipped off the bed?'

'I put it in his hands. If it slipped off the bed, Nicky might have put it in the closet after that.'

'I wonder.' Homer looked at his hands and pulled out a handkerchief to wipe the ink off his fingers. 'Damn pen leaks.' Then he bounced into the bathroom again.

'Look here, Hank. Nicky did write last night, after all.'

He had pulled back the long sleeve and disclosed Nicky's right hand. There was a small blue stain on the side of the middle finger.

'He was writing for quite a while. You'll notice that the stain isn't local. Nicky didn't notice the leaky pen. It dripped down his finger. There must be a stain on the sheet. He kept writing until he got sleepy. Then he dropped the notes into his briefcase until the thought of suicide struck him. He returned the briefcases to the closet, went into the bathroom, burned the notes — along with the Shipley notes — and then committed suicide. Sound logical?'

'Could be.'

There was the sound of a car

scrunching up the driveway.

'That's Swink and the coroner, Hank. Let them in through the back door. And be quiet about it.'

★ ★ ★

The coroner, a meaty little fellow named Bruck, gaped up at Nicky English. He pushed his glasses back on his bumpy forehead and tsk-tsked sadly, as though Nicky might have been an old friend.

Homer borrowed the coroner's tape measure, crawled around in the tub, fussed with the corpse and made rapid entries in his little black book. He measured everything — the stool, the shower rod and the width of the tub. He straddled the tub edge and dropped the tape from Nicky's head to the stool.

'What does it read, Hank?'

'Five foot five.'

'Hold the tape at Nicky's heel now.'

'Five foot three.'

'Check it again.'

I tried hard to avoid touching Nicky.

'Five three and one-eighth,' I amended.

'A small size coffin,' said Bruck. 'What you measurin' for, Bull?'

'I like to measure, Bruck. It's been pretty well proven that a suicide is more or less wacky at the moment of jumping off, hasn't it?'

'So I've heard. Never did take much stock in that sort of talk, myself. Man who commits suicide is a dern fool, yes. But he's far from crazy, the way I see it.'

'But doesn't a suicide usually manage the business with a certain neatness? He's thought the thing through, hasn't he?'

'Don't follow you, Bull.'

'Nor I,' said Swink.

'Here's what I mean,' said Homer with a smile. 'Nicky measures exactly five feet three and one-eighth. The distance from the stool to Nicky's head is exactly five feet five inches. That means that Nicky stood on his toes to tie the rope around his neck, doesn't it?'

Bruck looked up from polishing his glasses. 'Possible.'

'I won't argue the point,' said Homer. 'But it seems to me that a man who contemplated stepping off a stool would stand on it squarely. There'd be no reason on earth for Nicky to stand on his toes and tie that knot around his neck.'

'On the other hand,' said Swink, 'supposin' he tied the rope to the shower fixture first? It's possible that way, ain't it?'

'Is it, Swink? Would a man deliberately tie a knot around his neck so high that he'd have to stand on his toes? That'd be more torture, I should think, than suicide itself.'

Bruck studied the hanging figure quietly. 'Let's take the man down first, Bull, and argue later. I want to look at his neck.'

They were soon standing in the doorway, Bruck wiping his forehead, Homer and Swink awaiting his judgment.

'Far as I can see, Bull, the man choked to death. Neck wasn't broken — just throttled himself. He wound that cord round his neck so tight, I'd say 'twas over pretty quick after he kicked that stool away.'

'Wouldn't it be natural for his neck to break?'

'Not at all. Depends on the distance he dropped, I reckon. Man like this'd have to drop a good distance to break his neck, I'd say — him bein' so light and all.'

'You've had similar cases, then?'

Bruck nodded. 'Some. Fact is, most of 'em died the way this 'un did.'

'How about the rope, then? Have you ever found a knot on a suicide as unusual as this one?'

Bruck looked back at the john. 'How d'you mean, 'unusual'?'

'I'm talking about suicide knots exclusively,' Homer explained. 'They've always interested me, these knots that drag a weary soul into the next world. How would a man determine the knot he uses? It seems to me, allowing for the fixed and frenzied purpose of a man contemplating suicide, that he'd only tie a knot he'd tied before. Isn't that so?'

Bruck exchanged a baffled look with Swink.

'My point is this, gentlemen. I don't think we can find much variation in the type of knot a man will use to throttle himself. It stands to reason that habit would govern all knot tying in cases of this sort, doesn't it? A sailor might strangle himself with a half hitch, or a bowie, or whatever it is that sailors use for knotting most things securely. A cowboy, on the other hand, might tie another knot on his throat. So might a woodsman. But for most of us, knot tying involves the simple mechanics used in tying a Christmas package — one, two, three and it's done. Nicky English wasn't a Boy Scout. Nicky's knowledge of knots was limited to the colloquial. Do I make myself clear?'

There was a long pause full of wonder, curiosity and befuddlement.

Homer scooted into the bathroom and returned with the tape measure. He stood away from his audience, in the manner of an amateur Houdini about to do a card trick.

'This is what I mean. I'm about to commit suicide. Do I do this with my rope?'

He wound the tape three times around his neck and began to tie a knot under his ear.

Bruck came alive. 'You mean the

second and third time around the neck isn't natural.'

Homer tossed him the tape. 'Try it for yourself.'

Bruck stared at the tape measure for a moment. Then he looped it around his neck just once and tied a double knot.

'That's the way I'd do it.'

'You know nothing at all about knots, Bruck?'

'Know a few surgical knots. But I haven't used 'em in years now.'

'Yet you tied the simplest knot in the world on your neck just now.'

'I think I see your point,' said Bruck, pointing to his throat. 'You see, Jesse — this'd be the natural knot for the man to tie.'

Swink snorted. 'Fiddlesticks! I admit he might have tied it that way. You're splitting hairs, Bull. He might have shot himself, or stabbed himself, or drunk a bottle of iodine!'

'I love to split hairs, Swink. I've got another hair to split with you.' He held up the door key. 'I found this in English's robe.'

'Why not?' Swink was testy.

'What does it mean? Man wants to commit suicide. He locks the door, puts the key in his pocket and steps off the stool into paradise. How does that strike you?'

'It's possible, ain't it?'

'Of course it's possible, Swink. But are we searching for the possible or the probable? Why not continue on the trail of things normal?'

'Well, then, 'normal',' snapped Swink. 'Mebbe normal a couple of other ways, too. He might have left the hall door unlocked and locked himself in the john. He might have locked both doors. He might have locked the door to the hall and thrown the key out of the window.'

'Or left 'em both open,' Bruck suggested. 'A man like this, killing himself early in the morning, isn't afraid of any interference, now is he?'

'Variations of the same theme, Bruck. But I think you're nearer the truth, at that. Can't we rationalize and say that it would have been most normal for English to simply *lock* that hall door and *leave the*

244

key in the lock?'

There was a flash of agreement in Bruck's eyes. But Swink was stubborn.

'Look here, Bull. What're you gettin' at?'

'What do you think?'

'You think this man was murdered, mebbe?'

'I'm sure of it, Swink!'

18

Artful Gavano

Homer displayed the burned notes, the charred scrap, the leaky fountain pen and the briefcase.

'Somebody wanted us to think this a clear-cut case of suicide,' said Homer. 'But the evidence of suicide smells. We have all sorts of clues to suicide, pointing in several directions. The key is meaningless — all the locks are alike on this floor. But had Nicky left his key in the door, it would mean that nobody could have forced it out, even with another key that fitted the same lock. Number two is the rope. The rope is arguing that he hung himself, yet the knot betrays the possibility that he didn't hang himself at all. Number three: the burned notes. Why did Nicky burn them? Are they trying to tell us that Nicky might have murdered Shipley? Did he? I've never suspected

Nicky English of Shipley's murder.'

Swink was incredulous. 'Are you saying you know Shipley was murdered?'

'I'm not sure yet.'

'But — but this here note business. Maybe in them notes Shipley knew all along that English was out to get him!'

'Perhaps. I can't be sure of that either. Not yet. I'll know for certain tomorrow whether English had such a reason. The burned papers tell us nothing about Shipley's fears. How are we to know how many others among the guests Shipley feared? We're assuming that Nicky was the only one. We may be wrong.'

'Hair-splittin' again,' said Swink.

'You're wrong, Jesse!' Bruck was annoyed with the sheriff. 'Bull may be as right as rain. You're being stubborn. I kind of feel now there's a fifty-fifty chance this man here didn't commit suicide after all.'

'If he didn't, who in tarnation killed him?'

'I'm not quite sure,' said Homer.

'Then you suspect somebody already?'

'I suspect everybody, just now. But

there's only one way to find out, Swink.'

'Only one way? What's that?'

'You must cooperate with me. I want you to keep this suicide quiet until I give you the word.'

The sheriff pulled at his mustache. 'Quiet? How in tarnation you want me to do that?'

'Easily. You must take the body away with you right now.'

'Why now?'

'Well, you understand that if English was murdered, only one person in this house knows it. I think it's important to keep the suicide to ourselves for at least another day.'

'And then what?'

Homer chuckled. 'If I'm wrong, what are you losing, Swink?'

Swink turned to the coroner. 'All right with you, Hillary?'

'Right as rain!'

'Then let's go,' said Homer. 'I'll give you the signal to come down from the foot of the stairs. Hank, you and Swink carry Nicky down. We'll go out through the kitchen, into the garage. When you drive out, use the long way around, past the barn to the main road. I don't want to risk your being seen from the front of the house.'

I held Nicky by the legs and backed into the hall. Over Swink's shoulder, the first glimmer of dawn greyed the window at the far end of the corridor. I backed down slowly. My eyes hit the level of the top stair, and between Swink's legs I saw something far down at the end of the hall. It was a white speck moving. Perhaps the leg of a man's pajamas. Or a bit of a woman's lounging robe. Then I was down below the floor line. The speck of white had moved toward the right, probably disappearing beyond the wall leading off to the attic stairs.

Once in the garage, the frosty morning air smacked me wide awake. Swink eased the big car out slowly and quietly, and they disappeared behind the corner of the garage.

'Sleepy?' asked Homer.

I yawned in his face.

We were standing at the foot of the stairway when we heard the noise. A dull padding. Footfalls. Homer beat me to the top, but the hall was empty. He opened Nicky's door.

'I'll be spending the night in here, Hank. Get up early. I'll see you after breakfast.'

'Who do you suppose was snooping?' I whispered.

'Forget it. See you in the morning.'

I forgot it quickly. As soon as my head hit the pillow.

I decided to eat before visiting Eileen.

At eight o'clock I buttered another biscuit. That was number two.

Lester came in with a tray of dishes. He set things on the table slowly, in the manner of a trained ape with a set of toys. He couldn't see me. I enjoyed watching him.

Lester was muttering. You know the type. Broadway is rich with mutterers, some young, others old; thin, fat, moronic and hare-lipped. You see one walking toward you on the street, his mouth working over-time in a monologue. 'I'll break his goddam head,' says the mutterer, almost in your ears. You come to a semi-halt and stare at him. For the next block you ponder his problem. Break whose goddam head? Must have caught his wife with the milkman, you deduce. Or maybe his boss didn't come through with the raise he promised. You do not ponder long. You reach the next corner and the wind blows a skirt away from a smooth leg, tightening the dress around a muscular rump. So you forgot the mutterer. He probably was talking nonsense, anyway.

Was Lester talking nonsense? I caught a snatch.

' . . . skunk . . . might have known . . . ' he muttered, setting the plates in place ' . . . get even . . . '

His head shot up suddenly. I heard Mike Gavano's low-pitched whistle from somewhere back in the living room. Lester grumbled, put down his last dish and disappeared into the next room.

I got up and buttered another biscuit. This time I put some jelly on it. I returned to the chair, drew out a slice of scrap paper and made a note of Lester's mumblings. Maybe Homer would be interested. Little things seemed important after the session in Nicky's room. Maybe a goon like Lester muttered snatches that revealed the vacuum of his subconscious, or whatever it is the psychologists call the void in a goon's head.

I heard new voices, new whispers. They came from my left, just inside the living room.

A dame. Olympe!

A man. Who? I strained toward the screen until my head touched it, trying for his voice. It was low. Nevin? Or was it Cunningham?

I cupped my hand over my ear. That did it. Nevin's voice came through the screen in a whisper, low but clear.

'But after it's all over — ' (He seemed to be pleading.)

There was a long pause. No answer from Olympe. Her answer must have been written in her eyes, or in the shake of her blonde curls.

Nevin went on in the same tone. 'You can't mean it, Olympe . . . It's all past . . . forgotten . . . '

'Please . . . (Was she sobbing?) . . . Let's not talk about these things . . . Let's not talk about anything . . . not yet . . . '

She stopped abruptly. Somebody had interrupted them. A voice said: 'Morning, folks!' It was Cunningham.

Nevin and Olympe answered 'Hello' in almost the same breath, and they all moved off beyond earshot.

I reconstructed the dialogue on my piece of paper, trying for accuracy. I noted what I thought was most important — the fact that Nevin was pleading with Olympe. And Olympe — was she giving him the brushoff? What did he want? It would take a lot of something to make Nevin plead.

It hit me so suddenly that I almost laughed out loud. I wrote the word LOVE into my notes and put a question mark after it. Then I rubbed it out. Impossible. Nevin didn't seem the type to go for the imitation Dietrich. Or had I been seeing too many movies?

Somebody tapped me on the shoulder, and I tucked the notes away. Mike Gavano smiled his crooked smile, and the gold glittered in the sunlight. Mike was in a mood for fun.

'Playin' puss in the corner?'

I didn't answer.

'How's your noggin, chum?' He made a playful pass at my head, but I hit his hand down hard.

'I wouldn't hurt ya.' He grinned. 'You got a bad temper, sonny boy. You play rough.'

I stood up and said: 'I can play rougher.'

'A real fighter, ain't you, MacAndrew?'

'You said it. I've got a cracked conk that's sensitive to the laying on of hands. It annoys me, see?'

'Sure, sure. Oh, sure. How's Hawkshaw's dome? He all right?'

I nodded.

Gavano tapped my chest, right over the pocket. 'You been writin' mush notes, pal? Or was them funny pictures you was drawing?'

'Funny pictures. I'm always doing homework, Gavano.'

'Now ain't that dandy? Some day when I can afford the moola, you got to make my picture, pal. Ain't never had my puss done before.'

His stone-age profile was tempting. I pulled out a black litho pencil and a sheet of paper. Gavano stood as stiff as a tintype while I sketched in his contour in easy lines from the beetle brow to the jutting jaw.

Homer walked in and looked over my shoulder. 'An excellent beginning, Hank. I think you've captured the soul of your subject — the spirit of Pan on the loose.'

I said: 'You mean deadpan.'

Gavano rolled his eyes our way, but held his pose.

There was the sound of voices from inside, and Olympe walked out on the terrace, followed by Cunningham, Nevin and Trum. We moved in around the breakfast table, exchanging chit-chat.

Olympe parked opposite me. I couldn't help noticing her this morning. She had the edge on Grace. She overflowed with sex in a tweed rust skirt and a white sweater some libidinous designer must have created for the brassiere trade. In spite of this curvilinear display, it occurred to me suddenly that the woman was really beautiful. I mean her face. The phoney makeup had been abandoned on her dressing table. Her face held me. She had on a palish lipstick, laid lightly on the natural arc of her lips. I didn't mind the lips that way. I didn't mind her eyes any more, either. Yesterday's mascara had hidden their color. They were important, now, set in an unvarnished face. They shone. They were cold blue-green, yet soft and deep and lovely.

And today she matched her manner to her makeup.

Cunningham sat on her left, trying to talk with her, but the doll had changed, somehow. Her answers came low-pitched and hesitant. Something, some spark, had gone out inside her. Why?

19

The Ladies Speak Up

Eileen was glad to see me, and so was Nat.

'You're just in time for Dad's fourth cup of coffee,' she laughed. 'We have a perpetual breakfast here, you know. We're both fiends about coffee.'

'An old MacAndrew perversion. I've just finished my third up on the terrace. Never let it be said that a true MacAndrew spurned the fourth, fifth or sixth.'

'I'll make another potful in a jiffy, Hank. Of course, you'll have some more, won't you, Dad?'

'Just one, Eileen. It's a grand morning for chewin' the fat over the coffee cups.'

When Eileen went out, he whispered: 'Anything new up at the house?'

'Not a thing,' I lied. 'Guess we'll be leaving after tomorrow. That's if Bruck's satisfied.'

'Bruck's a plenty smart man, son. Reckon he's clever enough to know a suicide when he sees one.'

There was a silence while Nat loaded his pipe. Then he leaned over the table. 'What in tarnation ever brought him up to the house at four in the morning?'

'This morning?'

'Yep. Happened I couldn't sleep. Saw his car pull into the garage.'

I whistled in feigned amazement. 'That's funny. But maybe he came up to talk to Bull — might have been about the inquest, you know.'

'Inquest?' There was a quaver in his voice. 'What in tarnation for?'

'You've got me, Nat. Maybe I'm wrong.'

'Inquest,' he murmured. 'Can't understand it. That means more damned questions. Never could understand them things, anyhow. Legal business always was a mystery to me.'

Eileen answered the phone. 'It's Mr. Bull, Dad.'

I heard Nat ask: 'Right away, Mr. Bull?' and then he went for his coat. 'Be back soon, Eileen; Mr. Bull wants to talk to me.'

Eileen filled my cup. 'What's the first question, Hank?'

How could a woman be so smart and so pretty at the same time?

'What makes you think I'm going to ask questions?'

'Stop playing detective with me.' She smiled. 'Didn't Mr. Bull send you down here to question me?'

'You win. But that doesn't mean I wouldn't have come down here anyhow.'

She shook her head and I got a smile. 'I've only got a few questions, Eileen.'

'Go ahead, Professor Quiz!'

'Did you know that somebody came down here last night? To the backyard?'

A shadow of fear darkened her eyes. 'Down here? I don't understand.'

'There were a couple of visitors to the Tucker yard last night,' I said. 'I wondered whether you saw them hanging around.'

She seemed genuinely surprised. 'No, I didn't.'

'And just one more, Eileen — the last

one, I promise you. Did you go out skiing yesterday afternoon?'

'Yes. Why?'

'Where'd you go?'

'I started down the road, toward Woodstock. Then I — let's see — yes, I went over to the slope behind the house, by cutting across the big meadow. I stayed on the slope for about an hour or so. Then I skied back to the road and came home.'

'You didn't go up on the big hill?'

'Which big hill?'

'The one with the precipice — you know.' I pointed in the direction.

She got up petulantly. 'I don't get it, Hank! Don't you believe me? The barn's in exactly the opposite direction, and you know it!'

'I'm sorry, honey. That one was purely a personal question, strictly off the record.'

She eyed me quizzically. 'What do you mean?'

I leaned over the table until my hands touched hers. 'Homer didn't tell me to ask you whether you were skiing, honey.'

'Then why did you ask?'

This time I blushed. 'It's — well — I wanted to know whether you were up on that hill with a certain guy — somebody up at the house. I found a cigarette up there, with lipstick marks on it. I thought maybe you — '

Her laugh was low and sweet. 'A fine detective you are, Hank. Didn't you notice that I never use lipstick?' She paused. 'Unless you think that I prettied myself up for Mr. Whatshisname?'

She had read my mind. I said: 'MacAndrew is a dope.'

'MacAndrew is a funny man. Who did you think I might have met up on the hill?'

'Nevin.'

'Silly Billy! You might have gotten some information if you'd asked me that question a different way.'

'Don't rub it in, honey. What do you mean?'

'I mean that I know a little bit about who might have gone up on the Pine Hill yesterday. I was out in the backyard at the time. I saw her.'

'Who?'

'Olympe Deming.'

I kicked myself in the pants mentally. 'You're sure she went up to that precipice?'

'Almost positive. She started up toward the grove trail. The grove trail's the easier ascent to that precipice up on Pine Hill — it's more or less a beginner's trail. It parallels the Pine Hill Trail, then joins it on the last summit.'

'You didn't see Nevin?'

She shook her head. 'No. But I'm sure I saw Olympe, unless somebody was wearing her ski togs.'

I bounced to my feet. Eileen saw me to the door.

'MacAndrew feels better,' I said. 'You aren't mad at me?'

She squeezed my hand. 'Off the record, no.'

'I can return for a few dozen encores of java?'

'MacAndrew is always welcome.' She smiled. 'So long as he brings Hank with him.'

I made a quick grab for Eileen, and

before she knew it I had kissed her smack on the mouth, long and hard.

She didn't mind. So I kissed her again. Then I walked back to the house, whistling through my teeth.

I found Homer down at the end of the table, on the terrace. He was sitting with an electric percolator, a half-filled cup of coffee, and Olympe Deming.

'MacAndrew is back,' I said. 'Mind if I look over your shoulder while you work?'

Homer waved me to a chair. Olympe rose nervously and turned to leave.

'Please don't go, Olympe.' Homer was on his feet. 'I'll have Hank leave if it'll make you feel any better.'

'I'll go quickly, officer,' I said. 'What is there about me that frightens women?'

Olympe smiled weakly and paused at the door. 'It's quite all right, Mr. Bull. Perhaps later — I'll talk to you later.' She gave me a friendly grin. 'And you don't frighten me a bit.'

I bowed. 'MacAndrew is overjoyed.'

Homer flipped the pages of his little black book. 'A fascinating woman, Olympe.'

'What's eating her, Homer?'

'The jitters. The ladies all come to Father Bull, sonny. I ease their troubled souls; I comfort them in their hour of travail.'

I filled Olympe's empty cup. 'Meaning which?'

'The little lady is frightened, Hank.'

'What's bothering her?'

'I don't know. The little lady has changed, somehow — you've probably noticed. When a gal like Olympe suddenly changes character, remakes her personality, something's hit her — and hard!'

'I noticed that, Homer. She hit me the same way at the breakfast table, but I thought it had something to do with the bit of dialogue I overheard this morning.' I read my notes back to Bull. 'Does it fit?' I asked.

'Can't tell yet. But it might — it might, at that. I'm sorry I didn't hear about this sooner. I might have asked her a few questions about Nevin when I had her in the mood.' He added my straws to his little black book. 'How did it strike you, Hank? Give you any ideas?'

I said: 'Love. Is that possible?'

'Why not? But what made you think it was love?'

'The way Nevin spoke to her, mostly.'

'How do you know? Did you see him?'

'I told you I didn't see him or Olympe. I got all this through the screen. It was like closing your eyes at a movie.'

'Could be. He might have fallen for her.'

I made a face, a puzzled face. 'You really think that Nevin would go for a doll like her?'

'What makes you think Nevin doesn't like sweaters as much as you do?'

'I never said that she wasn't attractive,' I protested. 'But I wouldn't trust her as far as she can throw her chest.'

Homer beamed into my eyes. 'You're prejudiced, sonny.'

I blushed. 'Probably. Anyhow, I'll answer your question — I never did believe in women's intuition. Coming from Olympe Deming, I believe in it less.'

'She baffles me, Hank. I have an idea she's hiding something. It happened this way: I remained with my coffee after the others left the table. There were many interesting entries for my little black book. In the first place, nobody mentioned Nicky English until the little breakfast party almost broke up. Then Gavano made some crack about 'the keyhole Kid.' He wanted to know where Nicky was. Nobody paid much attention to his question — they were on their way out of the room at the time. Then Gavano and I were alone. Mike said: 'Nicky didn't take it on the lam last night, did he?' I told him that Nicky would surely be down later — that I had seen him in the hall this morning. Gavano left.

'Then Olympe came back, pretending that she'd left her lipstick. She seemed very much upset about something. We had a chat, and I could see that she was play-acting at being casual. Then she sprang the intuition gag on me. I told her that I believed in the guff thoroughly. She used it as a preface to a question. Olympe softened and changed completely. I have an idea that she's not as bad a dame as you think, Hank. Anyhow, she went on to tell me that the affair between Nicky and Cunningham last night had kept her awake all night long. She was worried — you'll die laughing at this — about Nicky English!

'She explained it simply. You see, after the scuffle on the stairs with Cunningham, Olympe couldn't sleep. She went to her room and read far into the morning. Then the old intuition began to work overtime. She commenced to worry about Nicky. She decided that she'd check up on the lad to see that he was all right. She came down the hall, she tells me, and when she turned the corner from her room, she saw a man leaving Nicky's room.'

'Of course she did! That was Jesse Swink's back she saw. She must have been the person I spotted through Jesse's legs when we were carrying Nicky out.'

'She was, indeed. She was also the person we heard when we were standing in the hall. She admits it.'

'What did you tell her?'

'I explained that the man she saw leaving Nicky's room was yours truly. Told her I'd gone into Nicky's for the same reason — to check up — found him okay, and left him after a few moments.'

'Did she believe you?'

'I don't think so,' he sighed. 'And I wish that I could believe her.'

20

Homer Diagnoses

Homer sat on the floor in the center of the studio, peering unseeingly up at the rafters. The cigar rolled along his lower lip in a slow-motion seesaw.

'How about the Shtunk's wire?' I asked. 'Aren't you interested?' Western Union had phoned almost an hour ago, from Woodstock. They had a telegram — a long telegram from New York. But Homer didn't even have the woman read it over the phone. 'You told her you'd be down for it soon.'

'It can wait,' he murmured without turning his head. 'Funny about this room, Hank. You know, I met Shipley only once or twice. Never really knew him at all. But this room, overstuffed as it is with bad furniture, is trying awfully hard to speak to me, to tell me just a little bit more about Shipley. I've had that feeling ever since the moment we walked in with Swink.

'This studio has told us a lot,' he went on. 'We know, for instance, that Shipley enjoyed light. He cut away three walls, instead of the usual north window. Yet, paradoxically, he enjoyed the darkness, too. Why else would he have only one lamp in the room — one reading lamp? You're an artist — how many lamps do you have in your room?'

'Three. And an extra lamp for my drawing table.'

'Yet Shipley had one. Then there's the big desk. Probably some high-pressure interior decorator sold him that item as Napoleon's office furniture. At heart, Shipley didn't care much for all this fluff. Else why should he fill that monstrous desk with bills and art supplies and all the unimportant junk a man collects around a studio? No, I have an idea that Shipley was quite normal at heart.'

For a long time he leaned on his fat hands, and I watched the smoke curl up in lazy lines from his inactive cigar. When he finally wriggled to his feet, a change had come over him. His eyes came alive with a sudden urgency.

'Get the car, Hank — we're off to Woodstock.' He snubbed his cigar end to a violent death. 'But first, a few minutes with Nat Tucker.'

We met Nat on his front porch.

'Which way to Doctor Butler's, Nat?' Homer asked.

'He's down past the first tea room, on the right side of the road, Mr. Bull. You feelin' sick?'

'Never felt better in my life, Nat. It's MacAndrew. He's got a dark green taste in his mouth. You going to be around here for a while? Want to do me a favor?'

Nat nodded.

'Keep your eye on the house, Nat. I'm anxious to know whether any of the guests leave during the day.'

Tucker squinted toward the main house. 'I can only cover the front door from here, of course. You want me to watch the road out past the barn, too?'

'If you can. I'll be back soon. Be too much trouble for you to sort of walk around the place every now and then?'

'Not at all, not at all.' He sniffed the air. 'Unless it snows.'

In the Western Union office, the buck-toothed operator grinned at Homer.

I read the message over Homer's shoulder:

DON'T GET SORE READ THIS FIRST YOU'LL SEE WHY STOP SEEN BLACK-WELL LAST NIGHT NICE GUY STOP KNEW NICKY WELL SAYS NICKY MARIE PARRISH STUFF MCCOY STOP ALSO NICKY INTENDED MARRY THE DAME STOP CHAUFFEUR PICKED MARIE UP THAT NIGHT DIDN'T KNOW WHOSE STOP ALSO COULDN'T SWIM STOP WILKINSON SAYS CASE WHITEWASHED BY TRUM STOP COMMISSIONER AT TIME PAL OF TRUM STOP KNOWS NOTHING ABOUT NICKY ENGLISH OR OTHERS BUT HAS STUFF ON LESTER MINTON EX CON FRIEND MIKE GAVANO ALSO STOP LESTER OKAY SINCE FOUR YEARS AGO AFTER LEFT PINDO STOP CUNNINGHAM OKAY FOUND NOTH-ING STOP TRACED OLYMPE DEMING AT POWERS AGENCY FOUND WOMEN

WHO KNEW HER STOP THEY SAY SHE
WENT WITH GUY FOR QUITE AWHILE
STOP THEY DIDN'T KNOW NAME OF
GUY BUT SAY HES YOUNG GOOD
LOOKER STOP HOME ADDRESS AT
POWERS CHECKED FOUND PARENTS
SPOKE TO THEM ON PHONE THEY
HAVEN'T SEEN HER LONG TIME
THOUGHT SHE WAS MARRIED STOP
SPOKE WOMAN SAYS OLYMPE BOY-
FRIEND NAME NEVIN STOP ANOTHER
WOMAN SAYS SHE THOUGHT GINK
NAME IS CUNNINGHAM ON ACCOUNT
OVERHEARD PHONE CALL ONCE STOP
CHECKED GAVANO ALSO STOP WAS
RIGHT ABOUT PLACE IN MALVERNE
ALSO ABOUT TINA ON ACCOUNT
CHECKED WITH BADER HE KNOWS
EVERYTHING STOP GOT IN NEVIN
PLACE JOINT FULL BOOKS BOOKS
BOOKS ALSO FEW SHIPLEY PAINT-
INGS STOP NOW AT SCARSDALE
LAST STOP

SHTUNK

Homer shook his head and wrote:

BREAK IN WIRE RESULTS IMMEDI-
ATELY

BULL

'If there's an answer, bring it up to
Tucker's, sonny,' he said. 'And now, on
to the good Doctor Butler.'

The good Doctor Butler lived in a big
house adjoining the Russian Samovar,
and the good doctor was at home. He
greeted us briskly.

'What happened to the man in the bandages? I thought surely he'd be well enough
to get down here today. Anything wrong?'

'Everything. The doctor bandaged, the
operation was a huge success, but the
patient died.'

Butler was aghast. 'Incredible! I thought
he was all right last night — at least, that
is — when did he die?'

'This morning. He was a suicide!'

'No! But that seems preposterous.'

Homer passed him a cigar. 'That's just
why I came down to see you, Doctor. I
was wondering whether that sedative could
have induced a state of melancholia.'

'Melancholia?' The doctor laughed

grimly. 'Unheard of. That was a simple sleeping powder.'

'How long before he'd wake again?'

'Not before morning, unless he were in severe pain.' Doctor Butler frowned. 'But even if that fellow were up, I find it hard to believe he'd kill himself.'

Homer made a check mark in his book. 'Did you ever have occasion to treat Shipley, Doctor Butler?'

'Once — but only in a — ah — minor way.'

'Then you never examined him?'

'Well, not exactly. He called me up to his place after a — ah — drinking bout. His stomach, you know.'

'How long ago was that?'

Doctor Butler scratched his nose. 'I can check on the date easily enough.' He turned in his chair and drew a white card from his filing cabinet. 'It was in the fall of '39 — three years ago.'

'And you haven't a record of any examination?'

The doctor colored. 'What are you getting at? I see no reason for exposing Shipley's record. It's unethical.'

'I'm sorry,' said Homer, smiling. 'I didn't want to violate your professional practices, Doctor Butler. I should have told you I knew.'

'Knew?' He frowned. 'Knew what?'

'That Shipley had an incurable disease.'

The grey eyebrows rose. 'But how? Don't tell me you detectives have become amateur diagnosticians?'

Homer beamed. 'Not at all. I had access to Doctor Torrance's file.'

'You had — access?'

'Doctor Torrance is away in Florida, you see. I knew that he'd been visited by Shipley not so long ago — a stub in Shipley's checkbook told me, so I wanted to know why Shipley went to him.'

'Yes,' sighed the doctor. 'Shipley had an incurable disease. But what can that mean to you?'

'It might mean a great deal.'

'Are you trying to discover, then, the reason for Shipley's suicide?'

'His condition was hopeless, wasn't it?'

'I didn't have his full record. But from what I saw — ' Butler shrugged.

'Did he seem to you the type of man

who'd kill himself for that reason?'

'I can't answer that, Bull. I didn't know him well enough. I saw him from time to time in the village. I don't remember that it ever affected his usual good spirits. He always seemed — well, normal. I should think a man like Shipley, an artist, might lose himself in his work and carry on. Shipley loved life.'

'Then you agree with me, Doctor Butler. You don't think the disease caused the suicide?'

'Hold on! I didn't say that.'

'I think,' said Homer, 'that Shipley would have waited for that natural death.'

Doctor Butler eyed him quizzically. 'You mean you doubt that he committed suicide?'

'I know it. Shipley was murdered!'

'Eh?' The doctor was amazed. 'Are you sure? How can that be possible? You think that one of his guests — '

'I'm sure of it. And it's almost my fault that another guest was murdered last night. I should have studied Doctor Torrance's card then, you see. Perhaps I would have called to ask you a few questions, Doctor.'

'I don't understand. You found something important on the card?'

Homer nodded. 'Only a word. But I didn't look for it in the dictionary until this morning.'

There was a long silence.

'A word?' asked Butler. 'What was that?'

'Amblyopia.'

'Eh? Really? Torrance found that?'

'Four years ago.'

The telephone dinged.

Homer rose abruptly and said goodbye. 'I may have some interesting news for you later, Doctor. Thanks for your help.'

In the car, Homer was still.

'Amblyopia?' I asked. 'What's that?'

'Dimness of vision.' He shot into gear. 'A one-word description of Homer Bull. But now it's my turn!'

'Your turn? I wish I could follow you. This thing gets more involved — '

'It's clearing, Hank. The whole stinking mess is ready for the funny sheets. All I need now is a climax.'

'Climax?' I gulped. 'Don't tell me it's

all over but the handcuffs?'

Homer bent over the wheel grimly. 'I won't tell you anything but this, sonny — we've got to move fast!'

'Must we move faster than fifty in this weather?' I gurgled. 'You'll wind up smeared against an oak. What's the hurry?'

'There may be another murder!' he whispered.

Homer chewed viciously on his half-inch butt and stared ahead into the greying snow. I knew now that the solution lay unraveled before him. He had put the last piece into its proper place.

21

Homer Smells Homicide

I skipped up the steps of the Tucker porch right behind Homer. Nat was in.

'Has Swink been up here?' Homer snapped. 'No? Get him on the phone, Hank. Tell him to come up pronto and to bring Bruck — and a deputy, if he can get one! Anybody leave the house, Nat?'

'Not until ten thirty, Mr. Bull. I just couldn't stay out after that. The snow — '

'You've been in since ten thirty?'

'I been sittin' near the window. Nobody could have got past here — '

'Nonsense!' Homer plopped his hat on askew. 'Somebody might have left the other way — past the barn.'

I said: 'Swink'll be up right away.'

'Call the house. I want to speak to Olympe Deming!'

Lester answered. Olympe wasn't around, he told me.

'Run up to her room, Lester! If she isn't there, let me know on the upstairs phone.' There was a silence. Then: 'She's not there either? All right.'

'Did you watch the rear of the house, Nat?'

'Walked 'round there at least four times.'

'Stay in back long?'

'Few minutes, I'd say.'

'Ah. Fine.' Homer seemed relieved. 'Then somebody could have come out the front door or the terrace and reached this house while you were around the back?'

Nat scratched his mustache. 'It's possible.'

Homer turned to me. 'Run up to the house and check on all the others, Hank! Don't come back until you're sure where they are.'

I ran back to the house, slowing to a walk in the hall. There was the rustle of thumbed paper in the library. I poked my head in and saw Nevin flipping the pages of an art book.

'Hello!' I chirped. 'You seen Gavano around?'

His head shot up. I had startled him.

'Gavano? I wouldn't know where he is, MacAndrew. I've been in here alone for some time.'

Gavano was in the living room with Trum and Grace.

'Hello, honey,' said Grace. 'Busy? We were just about to start a bridge game.'

'Why don't you get Cunningham?' I asked. 'He's a fiend at the game.'

'He won't play,' said Trum. 'Has a headache.'

'Is he in his room? Maybe I can coax him into it.'

'He's been up there for two hours,' said Grace.

I said: 'I've got a swell bedside manner. Betcha I get him down.'

I knocked on Cunningham's door.

'Come in,' he said woefully.

He was on his back in bed, reading a book.

'How's your head, Cunningham?'

He put his fingers to his lips. 'You're a lousy detective, MacAndrew, and I'm a liar. A good book never gives me a headache. But certain people . . . ' He grinned and winked.

Lester and Minnie were in the kitchen.

'Why, if it ain't Mr. MacAndrew,' she chirruped. 'And lookin' very hungry, too, isn't he? You lookin' for a snack, lad?'

'You're an angel, Minnie.' I chucked her under her bony chin. 'But I'm not hungry, honest. You found Miss Deming yet, Lester?'

He shook his head dumbly.

'Have you seen her, Minnie?'

'Not since after breakfast, I haven't.'

I mouthed a boiled egg from the salad bowl and left by way of the garage. Eileen was climbing out of her car when I arrived at the Tuckers'. I whisked her up the steps and through the door.

Homer said: 'They all up there, Hank?'

I nodded.

'Fine. Where've you been, Eileen?'

'Down to town.'

'You took Olympe Deming to Kingston?'

She colored. 'I thought it was a secret. She seemed desperate, Mr. Bull — told me she just had to get to New York this afternoon. Did I do wrong?'

Homer kissed her on the brow. 'Wrong? I should say not. You probably saved her life. You saw her onto the train?'

'I didn't wait. She told me not to.'

I opened the door for Swink, Bruck and a deputy. 'What's up, Bull?' Swink asked.

'Plenty. But it'll have to wait for just a little while. Why don't you and Bruck go up to the place, gather our guest list in the studio and wait for me there? I don't think we'll need an inquest after all, Swink.'

'Eh? Well, all right, if you say so. How long'll you be down here?'

'Not very long.'

'Who bought the notes from you, Nat?'

Tucker whirled, hitting his boot against the copper kettle on the floor. 'Eh? What in tarnation you talkin' about?'

'Please, please.' Homer's voice had an edge. 'We haven't time for theatrics, Nat. I know you took the notes from Eileen's desk, and I'm not blaming you for trying to sell 'em.'

'You knew all the time?' Nat slumped into the rocking chair. His hands trembled on the chair arms. 'You won't tell Eileen, will you? You *can't* — '

'I won't tell a soul, Nat, I promise you. But I must know now who paid you for those notes. It was Nicky English, wasn't it?'

Nat's eyes were wet and big. 'He told me he'd never tell how he got 'em. I never thought English would — '

'Nicky kept his promise, Nat. He didn't tell me. Did he pay you much?'

Nat lowered his head. 'Paid me five thousand dollars. But I'll give it back, Mr. Bull. I'll give it back.'

'You'll keep it, Nat. English didn't expect a refund.'

'Sure,' I said. 'Nicky's got plenty — '

But Eileen came in with a tray of sandwiches and coffee to end my account of Nicky's financial holdings. Somebody knocked on the door, and Homer jumped to his feet. It was the Western Union boy.

'Here's another wire just come through from Scarsdale when I left the office.'

Homer ripped open the envelope, read the message and reached for his coat. 'Let's go, Hank!'

The party in the studio seemed casual enough, except for the presence of Lester and Minnie, who stood in a corner eyeing the others nervously. On the big couch sat Grace Lawrence and Trum, between them a small tray with two highballs. Mike Gavano leaned against the mahogany desk, biting a toothpick and spitting small pieces of wood over his right shoulder. Cunningham and Nevin held down the two straight-back chairs near the drawing table. Swink, Bruck and the deputy stood near the door.

I took the seat behind the big desk and watched Homer lean his fat bottom against the top and grin around the room.

'This is a strange climax for a weekend party,' he began. 'Our host has already taken his leave in a rather — ah, abrupt fashion. Another of the guests has left the happy group, too. We found him hanging by his neck this morning — a suicide.'

'English?' Gavano asked hoarsely.

'English.' Homer nodded, smiling into Mike's eyes. 'The last man in the world you'd ever expect to kill himself, eh, Mike?'

'Jeez!' said Mike.

'But I'm telling my story backwards,' said Homer. 'I should start from the beginning — from the time I knew that I, too, was included in the guest list. That was on Monday morning — yesterday. I'm sorry I didn't come up on Friday, when Shipley expected me. Perhaps all this trouble might have been avoided, had I been here. I'm sure I could have stopped this thing soon after I discovered why Shipley invited me, of all his most casual acquaintances, to such a party.

'There were two reasons for his having me here, as I figure it. Either he was afraid, and wanted the protection of a friend addicted to amateur sleuthing, or else he simply asked me up so that he might enjoy the byplay between Mr. Trum, myself and my — ah — ex-wife, Grace Lawrence. I prefer to think that Shipley asked me up for the latter reason. I really don't imagine he knew what was coming. Hugo was a simple soul in many ways. This invitation to Homer Bull was his idea of a practical joke — a sideshow for his own amusement.'

Trum squirmed in his seat. Grace studied the ice in her drink.

'At any rate, I came,' said Homer, smiling. 'And just in time for the aftermath of a suicide. I must confess that the suicide didn't interest me at all, at first. I was more intrigued by the peculiar choice of guests, and the odd personnel of Shipley's household. The first character to make me wonder was Olympe Deming. Why was she up here? She wasn't a secretary, obviously. What was she doing in this place? Posing for Shipley, perhaps? I couldn't begin to understand. I couldn't understand why you were here, either, Mike.'

Gavano leered. 'I was ast up here.'

'Of course you were, Mike. You told me that only yesterday — and I believed you. But I couldn't quite see you as — ah — the logical guest for a party such as this. Not immediately, I couldn't. By the same token, Trum, your mission, too, didn't quite make sense. Nor did Cunningham's. Nor — ' He studied the carpet. ' — did yours, Grace. These things puzzled me. I wondered about Nicky

English — Shipley's avowed enemy. I wondered about Lester Minton, and Minnie, too. Matter of fact, it was the incongruity among our cast of characters that inspired me to give thought to what might follow. Then I found out about the book Shipley had started, and things began to happen. Eileen redid the first chapter of the book from memory. MacAndrew and I were slugged in the studio. The transcribed chapter disappeared.

'The book notes puzzled me. It became clear, almost immediately, that there were two parts to Shipley's projected book. The first section was the dictated chapter, which Eileen was able to reconstruct very well. The second part of the book, then, became the mystery. Shipley had prepared a few dozen pages of notes, all in his own handwriting, and gave these to Eileen to be typed. Eileen never typed this section. As a matter of fact, she read very little of it. Thus, nobody knew what these handwritten notes contained.' He stared around the room with a thin smile. 'My deduction was simple after that point, for it was obvious now that only one person, the thief, knew what the handwritten notes contained.

'Thus, the broth began to thicken. Whoever hit me in the studio had unwittingly banged reason into my head. I knew now that somebody was afraid. Somebody feared that Eileen might have read the handwritten notes and included them in her transcription.'

'Wait a minute,' said Swink. 'You mean that the feller who stole the notes from the Tuckers might have been the man who slugged you in the studio?'

'Why not? If the thief feared the divulgence of the handwritten section, he would be interested in knowing whether Eileen had read 'em, wouldn't he?'

'On the other hand,' said Bruck, 'anybody else interested in the handwritten notes might have been the slugger.'

'You've hit it on the nose, Bruck! If Shipley's notes were scandalous, why shouldn't some of the others who might be involved want to know where they stood? Any one of the guests could have slugged us.'

Bruck interrupted. 'Why should anybody be so all fired scared of Shipley's notes? Was the first chapter so bad?'

'Not at all, Bruck. The first chapter read like a True Confession story. But remember that our slugger didn't know these things.'

'Then he hadn't read that first chapter?'

'Who had? That chapter was dictated to Eileen. Only Shipley and Eileen knew its contents. But all knew that the Shipley book would be full of dirt. From then on, I began to look for motive. I reviewed the cast, with the help of an assistant in New York. From his information, anybody up here might have been the slugger in the studio. Nicky English had a very good reason for wanting the notes. Trum, too, was very much concerned. Cunningham might have — '

'That's a lie!' Cunningham snapped. 'I never cared a rap about Shipley's lousy book — and you know it, Bull!'

'All I know is what I read in the papers,' said Homer softly. 'But I'll admit that your motive would be weak,

Cunningham. After all, if you had done the job, it would have been in the line of business — you might have slugged us as a favor to Trum!'

Trum was red with rage. 'That's preposterous, Bull! Are you insinuating that — '

'Yes,' said Homer. 'I'm insinuating that you might have given your assignment to Cunningham and Gavano! After all, Trum, you've admitted to me that you were hell-bent on getting that stuff before publication. You also admitted a little deal with Gavano.'

'I called off Gavano! And I never told Cunningham to slug you, Bull. If he — '

'Never mind the 'ifs,' Trum!' Cunningham spoke sharply. 'I have an alibi. I was out in the snow at the time. Remember, Bull?'

Homer nodded. 'Your alibi is almost perfect, Cunningham, but it doesn't quite leave you in the clear. You had plenty of time to do the job, run through the main hall, grab your coat, leave the house and enter by way of the garage.' Cunningham half rose in his seat, but Homer waved him down. 'We're wandering away from the main line. I'll go back to my original statement. The man who slugged us in the studio was motivated by fear — a fear greater than any threat of blackmail.'

There followed a breathtaking silence. Mike Gavano spat the remains of his toothpick away and drummed on the desktop. Grace Lawrence gazed worshipfully into Homer's eyes, her buxom bosom heaving in three-quarter time. The circle of amazement included Swink.

'Worse than blackmail? What could that be now, Bull?'

'The person who struck us down in the studio was afraid of only one thing, Swink. There was a chance that the handwritten notes of Shipley's book *might brand him forever as a murderer!*'

'Eh? You mean Shipley knew this feller had killed a man?'

'Not at all. I mean that the text of Shipley's notes might have pointed to this person as *the murderer of Hugo Shipley!*'

22

An End and Two Beginnings

Homer drew the revolver from his pocket and faced his audience.

'I asked Sheriff Swink for this gun so that I might save my comic strip from the usual detective-story climax,' he said evenly. 'I'm an excellent shot. I don't want the murderer to escape. And if he leaps for this gun, I'll blow his brains out without batting an eye.'

Homer held the gun on his right knee, then raised it casually to point between Nevin's eyes. 'Here's your man, Swink. I don't think he'll make a sudden break for freedom!'

Homer was right, as usual. Nevin didn't move, didn't even look up.

Swink stepped forward. 'I oughta warn you, Nevin, that anything you say — '

'I know, I know,' said Nevin slowly.

'Mr. Bull is a fascinating storyteller. I prefer to listen.'

'Splendid!' said Homer. 'He has the sort of personality that will fascinate the alienists.'

Nevin smiled. 'A good suggestion, Bull — I'll remember that.'

'It won't save you, Nevin. You planned this murder calmly, with super-intelligent caution. But you made many mistakes.'

'Did I?' he said with a raised eyebrow.

'Far too many. You see, Swink, Nevin never intended to murder twice, but Nicky English forced his hand. And he might have killed a third time, if he'd known that Olympe Deming saw him enter Nicky's room shortly after midnight last night.'

Nevin's head shot up. 'Who told you that, Bull?'

'Olympe.'

'Jeez! Who woulda thunk it!' murmured Mike Gavano.

Nevin spoke to the handcuffs softly. 'You might have guessed it, Gavano. After all, if you had, I would have made you a new customer for blackmail, what with Hugo dead.'

'Whattaya mean, you lily-livered crud?'

'Come, come, Mike,' soothed Homer. 'You know Nevin's right. Are you denying you were taking dirty money from Shipley?'

'I don't have to answer, Bull! You ain't got no proof!'

'I can get it for you — wholesale!'

'Bright boy. How come you got so bright, Bull?'

'I was born bright, Mike. Hugo began to write a book — didn't you know? Didn't you know who he dedicated it to?'

'Yeah. Sure. He dedicated it to F.D.R. How should I know how he dedicates his book?'

'He dedicated it to you, Mike — his pal. For a while I thought that you were really the man who slugged us — that chapter certainly seemed to point your way. Shipley seemed fond of you.'

'Hugo and me was pals.'

'What did you ever do for him?'

'We was kids together. That's all.'

'Very noble, Mike. A pity your nobility wasn't real enough to have ruled out blackmail. I have an idea that Shipley shot a man once — long ago. I have an idea, too, that you saw him shoot.'

'You're nuts, Bull!'

'You're exactly right, Bull,' said Nevin. 'Hugo's told me the story. Gavano protected him nobly, until he met Hugo and discovered that he was earning big money.'

'He's lyin'! He can't prove nothin'!'

'I could,' said Homer. 'But I won't bother. The important thing is that you were blackmailing Shipley — and collecting enough to quit your rackets in Brooklyn, marry, and settle down.'

'Leave Tina outa this!'

'So far as I'm concerned, you're both out of it, Gavano. You worked your racket with Shipley very well indeed. I especially admire your system of self-protection — making doubly sure of your man by forcing him to accept your personal agent, Lester Minton.'

'Aw, cut it out, Bull — Lester ain't done nothin'!'

There was a soprano squeal from Minnie.

'Oh! I mighta known it! I mighta known that dirty dog was up to something with Lester!'

'Lester's no danger,' said Homer.

'Oh, I mighta known it!' Minnie held her head. 'Now it's jail. Now it's trouble for me! I've been a respectable woman; I served — '

'Lester's in no danger,' repeated Homer. 'He was only a watchdog, after all.'

'You don't know, Mr. Bull — he's no part of a dog, sir! He's more an ape!'

Homer nodded to the deputy, who led Lester and Minnie out of the room. He went on: 'Lester simply informed Mike of Shipley's activities. Last week, for instance, he managed to see the invitations to the weekend party and forwarded the information to Mike. That was the reason for my phone calls, wasn't it, Mike?'

Gavano sucked his toothpick.

'Mike was a little afraid that Shipley might hire a private detective to end the blackmail somehow. That started me up here. I dislike threats. Mike and your henchmen don't read the newspapers. They didn't see the item about Shipley's suicide, you know.'

Swink interrupted, waving a hand

impatiently. 'Never mind, Gavano. How'd you guess Nevin murdered the man?'

'That's what intrigues me,' said Nevin. 'There couldn't have been many clues.'

'Ah, but you're wrong, Nevin. You left many clues — important clues. My first look at the studio produced several. The most important, of course, was the information about the light. Everybody told me that there wasn't a light on in the studio when the body was found. Isn't that odd, Nevin?'

'Odd? Why?'

'After all, why should a man put out the lights before killing himself?'

'It's possible,' said Bruck.

'True — but it isn't normal, Bruck. And there were other clues. The easel was placed so that the light from the windows was useless. I examined the rug and found that it had been in that position for some time — there was a deep mark in the rug.'

'He might have worked only at night, honey,' Grace suggested.

'Yes, I know,' said Homer. 'But the easel had never been moved — not in a long time. It was a suggestion, at any rate. Then, too, there was the business of the paint tubes. They were all hardened.'

'Really?' said Nevin. 'You are clever, Bull.'

Homer bowed. 'Thank you again. These clues pointed to the fact that Shipley might not have worked in his studio for a long time — not in this studio, at any rate.'

'Of course!' I spouted. 'All that old French paper!'

'Stupid of me,' said Nevin. 'But of course I hadn't been up here in a long time.'

'What's all this got to do with the murder?' Swink massaged his scalp. 'For the life of me, I don't see how Nevin could have — '

'Nor do I, yet,' said Nevin.

'Nor did I — at first, Nevin,' said Homer. 'But I couldn't get that light business out of my mind. That was why I spent so much time in the dining room, staring at the spot where Shipley's body lay. I figured that there was only one way Shipley could have been murdered. The door was locked from the inside. You took a long chance, Nevin. You decided to remain inside the room, kill Hugo, lock the door and then hide somewhere until the door was forced in. Isn't that why you turned out the light after you killed him?'

Nevin nodded. 'Exactly. I needed time to jump from behind the drapes — ' He pointed to the south wall near the door. ' — look back into the dining room, and then walk in behind the others.'

'And it worked beautifully, Nevin. Lester broke the door in and ran to the body, followed by Minnie and Olympe Deming. You were about to jump out behind them when you heard somebody running through the dining room. You waited until Grace ran in, took another look and then followed Grace. Then you immediately lit the light, hoping in the confusion they might forget it had been out.'

'I'll be damned!' sang Grace. 'Now I remember that I didn't remember Nevin running behind me through the dining room.'

'Of course you didn't,' said Homer. 'And you'd never have thought twice about it unless somebody made a point of reminding you.'

'I had an alibi to cover that.' Nevin smiled wryly. 'I might have said that I entered by way of the other hall.'

'You might have, indeed, Nevin — but only after Nicky English died. Nicky English followed you into the room. If anybody at all saw you, it must have been Nicky!'

'It was Nicky,' said Nevin.

'I thought so, at the time. Nicky acted queerly. He seemed to be holding some information I needed. He wanted, he said, to 'break the story' through his own column. I imagine that Nicky saw Nevin step out from behind the drapes, but couldn't be quite sure of his man. Nicky was somewhere in the dining room at the time. He saw only a shadow moving forward into the studio. That was the reason for the unlit lamp, eh, Nevin?'

Nevin nodded.

Swink asked: 'Did you see English in the dining room, Nevin?'

'Oh, yes, sheriff. But too late to return to my hiding place.'

'So you decided to chance it — to wait to see how much Nicky really had seen. That was the reason for the second murder. You went to Nicky's room early this morning and found him asleep. On his bed you found several pages of notes, all written by Nicky. They practically named you as Shipley's murderer. There was only one way out, after that discovery — you strangled Nicky English.'

'Not at all,' Nevin said. 'I smothered him.'

'There were a good many clues, in spite of your pains, Nevin. You hung your man haphazardly. He would have had to stand on his toes to hang himself at that height. But you got the notes Shipley wrote in his own hand?'

'Burned them. My fears were stupid, Bull. I might have known that Hugo would never admit to using a — a stooge!'

'You didn't care for Shipley?'

'No, I didn't like him — I hated him!'

Homer chuckled. 'I'll have to give you a bit more fire, when I reproduce this in the comic strip, Nevin. I know a few of your reasons for killing Shipley. I discovered your background a while ago.'

'I suppose you found my home in Scarsdale?'

'Not immediately. I sent a friend to your office first. He observed a good many of Shipley's signed illustrations on the walls.'

'I'm a great admirer of my own artwork, Bull.'

'I knew that. I also knew that Shipley was a very sick man. That meant he was going blind. It also meant that he could no longer do any artwork. That's why he moved up here. I asked myself how Shipley could keep appearing in magazines, have an unused studio and yet do work. The answer was obvious — he was using a stooge. You were in love with Olympe, weren't you, Nevin?'

Nevin didn't say.

'I think you were,' said Homer. 'Olympe went out with you regularly when she worked for Powers. Probably posed for you, too. But she met Shipley and really fell in love with him. She begged him to tell you about it, you know. Even wrote him a letter asking him to explain it all to you. But Hugo never did tell you, did he?'

No answer from Nevin.

'So you decided to find out whether your suspicions were true. You missed Olympe. She had disappeared. You wanted her. You remembered, suddenly, that she had met Shipley. You decided to find out once and for all whether Olympe had come up here. You came up uninvited, on fire with jealousy. You watched the two of them, and it killed you to see how much she seemed to love him. So you planned to wait for him on Sunday night. It was a long wait. You walked into the studio almost immediately after dinner, hid behind the drapes, and watched the steady flow of traffic through Hugo's room. Finally she came in. There must have been a love scene. You waited until Olympe had gone, stepped from hiding, and killed him.'

'I should have killed them both.'

'I think Olympe felt that intuitively, Nevin. That's why she went away from this place. I've an idea she saw you leaving Nicky's.'

'I'm sure of it,' said Nevin.

'Olympe and I had a long talk this

morning. She seemed upset — nervous about Nicky English. Did she know you'd killed Nicky?'

Nevin shrugged. 'I suppose so.'

'And Shipley?'

'I told her about that.'

'Up on the hill?'

'You amaze me, Bull.'

'And you me, Nevin. Had you intended to kill Olympe?'

'Perhaps. Later, if she didn't come with me.'

'You're clever, Nevin,' Homer went on. 'I especially like your technique in robbery. I mean the way you managed to search Nicky's room without involving yourself. You upset Lester's room first, then searched Nicky's, then returned to your own, to victimize yourself. Weren't you surprised that Nicky didn't follow you upstairs when you said you wanted your pipe?'

'Not at all.'

'You're conceited. Nicky knew all along that you were rifling his room. He was giving you enough rope to hang yourself. If Nicky had spoken to me last night, he might be here now.'

I clicked the suitcase shut and sprawled on the bed.

'What I don't get, Homer, is this. I can't picture that guy Nevin slugging anybody. He doesn't have guts enough, it seems to me.'

'Guts? Those guys have plenty, in their own way.' Homer didn't look up. 'It was easy for him. He was behind the drapes when I walked in. He simply conked me before I switched on the lamp, searched me, jumped back behind the drapes when Lester came in, and repeated the job when you knelt over me.'

'A stinking mastermind. But how did he know where I hid the notes in the library?'

'That was a cinch, Hank. When we first met him, yesterday afternoon, do you remember the book you were reading? Nevin did — it was that yellow pornographic masterpiece. He must have known you'd favor that book over all the others, you lecher!'

There was a knock on the door and

Grace walked in.

'Are you ready, honey?'

'Ready and waiting, sugar!'

'Don't tell me,' I said, closing my eyes. 'MacAndrew is a sleuth. From the way you're dressed, I'd deduce that you're about to take a trip. Where? Elementary, my dear Watson. Isn't that the spark of madness gleaming in your big blue eyes, Homer?'

'MacAndrew hit it on the nose,' cooed Grace.

'And you're to be best man,' said Homer. 'Again.'

'This is where I came in eight years ago, Homer. Nope. MacAndrew stays on up here. Blessings on you, my children.'

I backed the car out of the garage and eased down the driveway.

Eileen met me at her door. 'You're not leaving, Hank?'

'MacAndrew is *back*,' I told her. 'Back for fifteen thousand cups of coffee.'

She didn't understand, at first.

But Eileen is plenty smart. I sold her the idea after ten minutes.

We do hope that you have enjoyed reading this large print book.

Did you know that all of our titles are available for purchase?

We publish a wide range of high quality large print books including:
**Romances, Mysteries, Classics
General Fiction
Non Fiction and Westerns**

Special interest titles available in large print are:
**The Little Oxford Dictionary
Music Book, Song Book
Hymn Book, Service Book**

Also available from us courtesy of Oxford University Press:
**Young Readers' Dictionary
(large print edition)
Young Readers' Thesaurus
(large print edition)**

For further information or a free brochure, please contact us at:
**Ulverscroft Large Print Books Ltd.,
The Green, Bradgate Road, Anstey,
Leicester, LE7 7FU, England.
Tel:** (00 44) **0116 236 4325**
Fax: (00 44) **0116 234 0205**

Other titles in the
Linford Mystery Library:

VILLAGE OF FEAR

Noel Lee

After narrowly escaping death on a train, two people find themselves in an eerie deserted village — and make a grisly discovery . . . On a dark and stormy night, locals gather in an inn to tell a frightening tale . . . A writer's country holiday gets off to a bad start when he finds a corpse in his cottage . . . And a death under the dryer at a fashionable hairdressing salon leads to several beneficiaries of the late lady's will falling under suspicion of murder . . .

PUNITIVE ACTION

John Robb

Soldiers of Fort Valeau, a Foreign Legion outpost, discover the mutilated bodies of several men from their overdue relief column, ambushed and massacred by Dylaks. Captain Monclaire's radio report to the garrison at Dini Sadazi results in a promise that more soldiers will be despatched to Valeau, from there to mount punitive action against the offenders. But before the reinforcements arrive, the Dylaks send a message to Monclaire — if he does not surrender, they will attack and conquer the fort . . .

DEATH WALKS SKID ROW

Michael Mallory

Sunset Boulevard, 1975: Two men are speeding home from a party on a night that will haunt them forever. Despite the dangerously wet roads, both passenger and driver are very drunk. Thirty years later on Los Angeles's Skid Row, a homeless man is found dead in an alley. Discovering several disturbing connections, reporter Ramona Rios and a man known on Skid Row only as 'the governor' set out on separate paths to unveil the truth, but are brought together to face a perilous web of power, manipulation and deceit.

ONCE YOU STOP, YOU'RE DEAD

Eaton K. Goldthwaite

The USS *Slocum* is on a routine naval patrol northwest of Bermuda when the SOS crackles over the radio. Cuban National Air's Flight Twelve is ditching in the Atlantic with eighty-nine passengers and five crew aboard. Commander H.P. Perry readies his ship for standard rescue operations — only to discover there's nothing standard about the survivors. Once aboard, they're more demanding than grateful, for most are Russian or Cuban nationals. That's when Commander Perry realizes he's an unwitting pawn in a deadly game, the outcome of which could have grave international repercussions . . .

MURDER GETS AROUND

Robert Sidney Bowen

Murder and mayhem begin innocently enough at the Rankins' cocktail party, where Gerry Barnes and his fiery red-haired girlfriend Paula Grant while away a few carefree hours. There, Gerry meets René DeFoe, who wishes to engage his services as a private investigator, for undisclosed reasons — an assignment Gerry reluctantly accepts. But the next morning, when Gerry enters his office to keep his appointment, he finds René murdered on the premises. He puts his own life at risk as he investigates why a corpse was made of his client . . .